Cadet David Forester Had an Exciting First Day at Starfleet Academy . . .

"The whine of the phasers cleared my head. I turned to the guy under me, gritted my teeth and got used to the idea of bashing a face in.

"Somebody grabbed my elbow, stopping my punch. I quickly freed my other hand and threw a punch at the person who was holding back my other arm. He twisted with the hit, but didn't go down. In fact, he held me tighter.

"I stared at him with sudden recognition. . . . My first day at the Academy, and I, David Forester, had just punched Captain James T. Kirk in the jaw. . . ."

STAR TREK®

STARFLEET ACADEMY®

A NOVEL BY DIANE CAREY

**BASED ON THE INTERPLAY PRODUCTIONS
CD-ROM *STARFLEET ACADEMY***

Written by
DIANE CAREY & SANDY FRIES &
DAN GREENBERG

with
RUSTY BUCHERT, SCOTT BENNIE,
STEVE PERRIN,
ANDREW GREENBERG, BILL MAXWELL,
BILL BRIDGES

POCKET BOOKS
New York London Toronto Sydney Tokyo Singapore

This book is a work of fiction. Names, characters, places and incidents are products of the author's imagination or are used fictitiously. Any resemblance to actual events or locales or persons, living or dead, is entirely coincidental.

POCKET BOOKS, a division of Simon & Schuster Inc.
1230 Avenue of the Americas, New York, NY 10020

This book is published by Pocket Books, a division of Simon & Schuster Inc., under exclusive license from Paramount Pictures.

ISBN: 0-671-01550-8

First Pocket Books printing June 1997

10 9 8 7 6 5 4 3 2 1

POCKET and colophon are registered trademarks of Simon & Schuster Inc.

Printed in the U.S.A.

STAR TREK®

STARFLEET ACADEMY®

Chapter 1

"Two years ago we again put out the call and challenged you to go where no man has gone before. I am Aex Rotherot, and as Commandant here I'm very proud to welcome you to Starfleet Academy Command School. Since Starfleet Academy was founded, the United Federation of Planets has sought the best and brightest from over a thousand worlds."

Boy, did we look fine.

Since I was three years old and my mother dug the grit of Earth out of my ears and scrubbed me pink, I never felt cleaner. Being a cadet at Starfleet Academy was breathtaking enough, but being accepted to the Command School—I almost flipped over the whole idea. Until now, it only had been a letter of acceptance tacked to my headboard, but today . . .

"David. David!"

"What?" I shook myself and looked at Robin. He had a shocky glaze on his cheeks. Did I look like that?

"You're slowing down," he told me. "Shouldn't you keep moving?"

I stepped up my pace in the long line of command cadets, but the splendor of this place admittedly socked me with a big awe and even bigger insecurity. The rafters were vaulting and snowy white, the thirty-foot backdrop curtain a shimmering electric blue, and the rows upon rows of seats covered in gold plush. White, blue, gold . . . Starfleet.

I thought I was going to go blind.

On either side of the auditorium were thirty-foot windows. To our right, we had a perfect view of the shimmering blue San Francisco Bay, which the curtains in here were meant to imitate. We could just see the Point Bonita Light standing sentinel as it had since the 1800s.

On our left sprawled the stately complex of Starfleet Command, its courtyards demarcated by formal sculpted boxwoods, and its hills jeweled with the Thomas Jefferson Rose Garden.

Somebody had done this on purpose—positioning this particular building right between those two overwhelming vistas, stationing Starfleet Academy right where we could train and study and sweat within sight of Starfleet Command.

And it was working.

On the main platform, commandant Rotherot paused in his introduction to give the queue of cadets a chance to finish filing into place and sitting down. I was almost in front—about three rows from the platform, and blinked into the natural sunlight brought down from a prism-ceiling that was meant to save power but also to imitate the deck prisms of old sailing ships, just so everyone would remember the roots of tradition here. This place was tradition to the gills, and as bright as the summer outside.

Just as I sat down, another officer, smaller statured than Rotherot and with slick black hair and an amused expression, climbed the short steps and joined the commandant on the platform.

"Robin!" I gasped abruptly. "That's Captain Sulu! I didn't expect him to be here!"

"Kinda wish I was someplace else too," Robin murmured.

I scolded him with a glance. "You've been saying that for days, but you're still here."

He looked at me nervously and tried to change the subject. "Didn't you tell me Captain James Kirk was supposed to be the keynote speaker."

Robin's problems melted out of my mind at the thought of what he had just said—

"James T. Kirk!" I said. "I hope he's still coming! Maybe we can shake his hand."

"Oh, no—I don't want to shake his hand! You're not going to make me, are you?"

Typical. Robin never wanted to be noticed. So while I was standing next to him, I wasn't supposed to be noticed either. That was his version of security.

Commandant Rotherot was still waiting for the last few cadets to settle down, using the moments to make sure the citations and pins on his chest were all straight and polished. He even licked his finger and pressed back a hair that really wasn't out of place, and the gesture hit me like a punch. Was *he* insecure too? Could that be? Did senior officers get nervous?

Then Rotherot noticed Captain Sulu watching him quizzically, amused, and he quit fidgeting.

"Don't you think we should get started, Commandant?" Captain Sulu asked—I could hear him from only three rows away. What a voice.

"He isn't here yet," Rotherot said.

Sulu smiled. "Jim Kirk hasn't missed a command school opening for eight years. He's gotten to where he enjoys them. He'll be here, so—"

The deep voice faded as Sulu turned to look at something and the sound went off in another direction.

What was going on? I looked around, but the only thing that happened was Rotherot taking the lectern rather nervously. The rest of the cadets took their seats behind me and Robin. We looked like a spirited investment in the future, and I was proud and—all right—terrified to be part of it. I wasn't one of those kids for whom Starfleet had been a known constant while I was growing up. In fact, I hadn't given the service a single thought until high school.

Then, one silly vacation with my eccentric uncle to a flight-sim camp, and I was hooked. I started driving everything, anything that would go. Rolling, flying, skimming, floating—I wanted to *go*.

Now, I was here.

Guess I *went*. Sometimes life could be a whirlwind.

The huge backdrop behind Rotherot startled me when it turned into a giant field of stars—a display screen of some kind, but big! And gorgeous . . .

Starfleet vessels of all types sailed by, vessels from the past, from the early days of exploration, clunky and strong ships that had taken the worst poundings space could offer. They reminded me in some ways of the Conestoga wagons used by pioneers. They seemed primitive and flimsy and easy to laugh down our noses at, but in fact they were well armed and tough enough to rattle across great expanses and actually get where they were going. For just a few seconds, I got lost back in time with them.

"David?" Robin's voice was distant, meaningless. "Something wrong?"

I didn't answer. The starships were starting to appear. The early classes of fleet ships built by the Federation once they established Starfleet as their exploratory and defensive arm. Just like the old time cavalry, they were the ones who went out and carved paths into the wilderness for settlers to come after. They'd established the forts, and people had gone out to connect the dots of the galaxy. Pretty soon, I'd be going.

The first of my family—a pretty big family at that—to join Starfleet . . . Everyone else went to Clark University.

Not like Robin. He had about five Starfleet servicemen in his family past. That's why he was here, in a place where he just didn't belong, facing a future that didn't fit him.

"Move aside, plebe," a mass of protoplasm barked on the other side of Robin.

I looked around in time to see this mass give Robin a subtle but firm shove with one sausagelike finger. A senior cadet towered over us, his shoulders cutting out light from the ceiling prisms.

"Out," the senior growled down at Robin.

"Hey." I stood up. "You got a problem?"

"No problem, except your pal is sitting in my girl's seat."

Girl? Was there a girl? Oh, yes—

"Not here, Frank." A female cadet appeared from behind the senior pulled on his meaty arm.

"Why don't you just ask politely for us to move down?"

"Because seniors don't 'ask,' that's why, junior."

"Frank, just sit down," the woman said.

I took Robin's arm and we shuffled down one seat, causing the whole row of cadets to shift like a choppy wave. Nobody made any protests—seemed some of them knew this guy.

Good thing, because I was ready to protect Robin, and that Frank could easily have separated my head from any related tissue.

Luckily, the senior let the girl move in and sit between him and Robin, but only after we moved down a seat so the pair of them had room to sit together. I'd heard about the strictness of senior cadets, for it was they and not officers who kept other cadets in line at command school.

At the lectern, Commandant Rotherot straightened his pins and medals one more time, then started talking again.

"Ladies and gentlemen, it's my proud duty to present the new head of the Command School—"

A loud whine blasted across the auditorium. At first

I thought it was an alarm of some kind, maybe a mistake by the backstage guys running that beautiful screen full of ships passing by, but all at once I noticed that half the field of cadets were ducking their heads.

Somebody shouted, "Down! Down!"

I twisted around to see what was happening—never occurred to me that the cadets might actually be ducking for a good reason—and a second whine broke across the auditorium so close that my right ear ached.

I cranked to my right.

A cadet at the back of the auditorium stood with legs braced, and in his hands was a phaser rifle!

A cadet—a Vulcan cadet.

Had a Vulcan snapped?

"I know him!" I said under the noise to Robin. "That's Sturek. I had a couple of computer classes with him last—"

Somebody yelled, "Look out!"

The Vulcan—Sturek—broke stance and rushed down the aisle toward the front platform.

Beside me, Robin craned around, too confused to duck. Past his startled face I saw an angry-looking human woman with brassy hair and an Andorian woman rush in from the wings, and they were firing some kind of projectile weapon at Commandant Rotherot!

The senior named Frank bolted to his feet, but froze in place, his arms flared at his sides. He wanted to do something, but seemed completely lost about *what* to do.

7

On the platform, Captain Sulu jumped in front of Rotherot and was driven down by the shots. I pushed to my feet and gripped the top of the seat in front of me, but that was as far as I got before a dark-skinned human about my age dropped from the ceiling—right out of the ceiling!—on some kind of cable.

Well, this was . . . what *was* this?

"David!" Robin's voice was suddenly behind me.

He hadn't moved. I had. I was standing on the back of the chair in front of me—launching off it, more like, and the platform was only a couple more jumps away, and that dark-skinned guy was just hitting the platform behind Sulu and Rotherot.

Behind me, the field of cadets was paralyzed with shock and horror as phasers sang across the auditorium, and I was pretty horrified to find myself rushing the stage. That dark-skinned guy was like a boxing sandbag when I hit him, but he went down just as his phaser rifle screamed against my ear. I must've hit him just right, because he outweighed me by a good thirty pounds and probably could've turned me into goop if I hadn't had the advantage of momentum.

The two women were rushing the platform now. Against their forms I noticed that the display screen had frozen with one ship halfway passed. One of the women stopped and aimed at Rotherot, but Sulu forced himself up and got her by both ankles. The platform shuddered beneath me as they crashed to it. He'd brought her down.

"Get off me!" the guy under me howled. I had his right arm pinned and the phaser rifle under my leg, but his left arm was free and he pummeled me freely in the head and shoulder. The only blow I felt in the midst of shoving this guy down was a whack on the ear that sent my head reeling.

Sturek loomed over me! I saw the flash of a phaser rifle and thought I was dead, but a new figure vaulted over me, skimming my right shoulder and caught a toe on my shoulder blade. The solid figure landed on one knee instead of both feet, but still managed to slam Sturek against the back wall.

Twisting to look, I saw a stocky Starfleet officer's thick arms strain in his uniform tunic. His face was flushed, his amber eyes hard—I knew those eyes. How many portraits had I see just in the past six weeks . . .

James Kirk!

Kirk smashed the Vulcan to the back of the stage, and the phaser rifle flew out and skittered to the deck inches from the hand of the guy I was holding down, distracting me for an instant—there were now two phaser rifles within a few inches of me. Could I get one? Should I?

The guy under me wasn't so doubtful. He surged up in a sudden gush of power and threw me off, and scrambled toward Sturek's phaser rifle.

"No!" I shouted, and plunged for his legs just as he got the rifle and rolled over.

I overshot and landed on his rib cage. He bawled in pain as my action nearly dislocated one of his shoulders, and he slammed into the stage deck, dragging me with him.

There was another uniform on the stage now, and I knew this one right off too. Commander Chekov. He was an instructor at the command school. He'd organized the cadets and given us our initial orientation not two hours ago. Now he was chasing down that Andorian woman and the human woman, who were both firing at him, but he managed to dodge them, and he had his own hand phaser with which he was keeping them from getting aim on the run. They were headed out of the auditorium.

Were they giving up? Or had Captain Sulu been the target of all this?

The whine of those phasers cleared my head. I turned to the guy under me. Even though I'd never even kicked a cat in my whole life, I pulled back a fist, gritted my teeth and got used to the idea of bashing a face in.

Somebody grabbed my elbow! I couldn't throw the punch—and I'd made up my mind to throw it. Furious and caught in the heat of insult, I freed my other hand and swung it instead, but around at the person who was holding back my arm. Contact!

Clipped him right in the mouth. Caught a knuckle on his tooth.

He twisted with the hit, but didn't go down. In fact, he held me tighter.

I stared until my eyes stung. I'd just clipped James Kirk in the jaw!

Chapter 2

Why was Captain Kirk holding me back? Wasn't he on my side?

The guy under me squirmed away, and for some reason I let him go.

Sulu rose behind Kirk like a Tahitian god. "Belay that, cadet!"

He was talking to me. I guess he thought I was going to throw another punch. I looked, and saw that my fist was balled up again, ready to go.

James Kirk shifted back and pulled me to my feet. "Good job. Stand down."

He turned to the field of stunned cadets, most of whom were on their feet by now. In contrast to Commandant Rotherot's fastidious neatness, Kirk didn't care that his maroon uniform jacket was rumpled and bunched, his hair disheveled, and his lip bleeding. He looked rough and didn't care. He yanked down the chest panel of his jacket, leaving the white lining showing, and let it hang that way.

His voice carried to the back of the hall.

"You've just seen an assassination by terrorists! How many attackers were there? How many got away? What were they wearing? Male or female? Human or not? And why did only one cadet take action?"

Rubbing his reddened jaw, he paused to let the questions ring, and turned to look at me.

I felt cold all over. Beside me, Sturek helped the dark-skinned guy to his feet.

Captain Kirk's questions rolled in my head—could I answer any of them?

The field of cadets glanced at each other, realizing they'd been had. Rotherot got up and checked his appearance. Commander Chekov strode down the main aisle with the two women at his sides. They seemed damned pleased with themselves.

Kirk nodded at Chekov, then looked at me.

"What's your name?" he asked.

"Uh—" I licked my lip, but that didn't help. "Um . . ."

He drew a long breath, giving me one more second, then insisted, "The name, right now."

"Uh—Cadet David Forester, sir."

Turning again to the audience, Kirk said, "Cadet Forester survived. The rest of you are dead. So is your commandant and your command school's senior captain." He motioned to Sulu and Rotherot. "Not good things to have on your headstones."

He moved away from me, forward on the stage,

until all eyes were fixed on him. His voice carried through the hall.

"Now you know that non-action has repercussions, just as action does. Sometimes a rash decision now is better than a thoughtful one five minutes from now. You're about to go into command training on the most technologically advanced simulators in the galaxy. Don't treat them like simulators. You never know what's real and what's not. What you learn at this Academy you'll be taking with you . . . out there."

He pointed upward, at the vaulted ceiling, at the sky, at space beyond both. The field of cadets looked up, and so did I, as if we could actually see space through James Kirk's eyes.

"And out there," his voice carried majestically, "everything's real. You answered the most profound call in history—commanding a Starship crew."

He paused as the backstage crew got the display screen moving again. The frozen ship passed on by, and blended into an aerial view of San Francisco, and Starfleet Headquarters.

Captain Kirk brought us down to Earth with a single step forward.

"Starting today," he said, "you better be ready. There are damned few second chances, but plenty of first ones. They'll fall on your shoulders. You'll be the ones to open the galaxy. You'll be Starfleet."

A moment of silence fell, chased soon by applause breaking out from the cadets like bells ringing. Another moment, and that applause blended with cheers.

Commandant Rotherot stepped forward to James Kirk's side, and motioned for the cadets to sit down.

My legs felt like rubber. I wasn't going to faint, was I? Did they want me to go back to my seat or what?

"Captain Sulu?" Commandant Rotherot gestured to the lectern.

"Sit down, everyone," the "assassinated" captain said as he took the lectern, and he paused a moment as the field of cadets uneasily lowered into their seats again. "I am Captain Hikaru Sulu. I'll be with you the next two years before I take command of the *U.S.S. Excelsior*."

Behind him, on the huge display screen, a view of Earth was decorated brilliantly by the passing of the great new class of starship in standard orbit. Heavy and complex, the *Excelsior* slowly passed in tribute to her future captain.

"It's my job," Sulu went on, "to create the Starfleet commanders of the future. I'll test you on your ability to manage your crew. Remember, you'll no longer be judged solely by your own conduct, but also by the conduct of those you command. And now, in case you don't already know . . . I'm privileged to present my friend, our distinguished guest . . . Captain James T. Kirk."

I stood aside as James Kirk took Sulu's place, as if none of this had happened at all! How could he be so—

My breath stuck in my throat when the big backdrop blended to a crisp, touchable vision of the new *Enterprise*—NCC1701-A. There was no mistaking that ship. Refit and sparkling, the fleet's flagship soared slowly past behind her famous captain. They were together right here in this room, before my very eyes.

What was I supposed to feel?

"Welcome to command school," James Kirk said, as casually as if none of the staged attack had happened at all. It was as if we all had a joke to share. "You've just embarked on the most challenging course the Academy has to offer, and also the most rewarding. It's often said that command cadets are the best of the best. And it's also said that I commanded the best ship and the best crew. You want to know the truth? There's no such thing as 'the best.' One ship may be brand new state-of-the-art technology, but it also might have countless bugs to work out. Another ship may be a hundred years old and shake like a rattle, but the bugs are long gone and that's why she's a hundred years old."

He paused, looked out over the field of command candidates, and his eyes twinkled with deep-laid tease. Behind him, the gorgeous new *Enterprise* passed by, and what came behind her choked up every throat and brought a tear to every eye . . . .

There, gigantic on the screen behind her captain, was Starfleet's greatest lady, the very first *Enterprise*, the oldest, the toughest, the one that had gone the farthest back when far was really far. She looked simple to us now, her muscular lines basic and her hull plates flashing like polished eggshells. Her red sensor disk was a target against the sky, or a pulsing heart against history.

The blood fell right out of my face. I was as white as that ship.

Now the ship faded away, replaced by a field of atmosphere-blue, and upon that was imposed the brassy delta shield symbol of Starfleet, with a brass ring around it as tall as the whole screen. There the display paused, and let Captain Kirk take over our complete attention.

"The same goes for your crew," he said, his voice mellow and captivating. "They may be technical wizards, but if they can't work as a team, their skills are useless to you. When you meet your crew you'll find a thousand abilities and talents and flaws all crackling against each other. And that's where you come in. Those of you who succeed in building a team will be among the elite few who take us to the stars. Good luck . . . fair weather . . . and never forget that risk is your business."

The hall full of cadets stared at him, overwhelmed. So did I. Was he telling us that all those "best and brightest" phrases were just wishful good publicity? That's what it sounded like—and he would know, wouldn't he?

I had the feeling we'd gotten the greatest advice we could be given in ten years of experience, and James Kirk had given it to us in ten sentences.

After a humbling pause, somebody way in back stood up and started applauding. Then, like rising tide, everybody did. Soon the hall was a sea of cheers.

I was still looking for my hands when Commandant Rotherot came forward again. "Cadets, you're dismissed to meet with your advisers. Good luck."

The rubber legs only shuddered when I tried to

move. Cold sweat skittered beneath my uniform. *That* wasn't very best or brightest.

A few steps from me, Captain Sulu moved up to Kirk's side with an evil grin. "Did you trip on purpose?"

"I'll never tell," James Kirk said with a smirk.

Commander Chekov hopped up onto the stage. "I love to watch the cadet's faces when we do something like this. I wish we could do it every year!"

"They'd wise up if we did," Kirk droned, unimpressed with himself. He pointed to me then, and I thought I'd been shot. "Captain Sulu, I want you to put that kid in charge of those kids."

Now he swung that pointing finger around to the Vulcan, the dark-skinned guy, and the two women. Maybe I was a little slow, but I was getting the idea that these were cadets too, snagged for their first undercover mission.

"Done," Sulu said bluntly.

Kirk turned and stepped right up to me, drilling me with the most unflinching eyes I'd ever seen. "Forester . . . good name. Gives you a lot to live up to."

Having no idea what he was talking about, I was afraid to agree. "Beg your pardon, sir?"

"The name Forester has been synonymous with high seas adventure since the first Horatio Hornblower novel. C. S. Forester taught me how to command a ship."

Oh, great! I stammered, "But that's not—!"

"Not fair having to live up to someone else's

reputation?" Kirk anticipated. His sharp eyes carried an undefined glint. "You bet it isn't. Just wait till you have to live up to your own. And by the way, next time try to hit the bad guys. Dismissed."

He turned away from me. Just like that. Just turned as if all this were nothing.

Robin tentatively climbed up onto the stage, keeping shy of the cluster of legendary men, and swerved to my side as if I could protect him from them.

He took my arm. "David, that was great! You all right?"

I choked up a voice to tell him I was fine, but something else squeaked out.

"I hit James Kirk . . . "

Four hours later, my stomach was still quivering and an echo looped in my head. *I hit James Kirk. I hit James Kirk . . . .*

"Cadet? This way."

A door panel slid open in front of me, and Commander Chekov gestured me through the entrance onto a gunmetal gray carpet. The first thing I noticed was the sanctuarial quiet of the setting.

Around me was a representation of the pulse of the settled galaxy—the bridge of a starship.

The breath left my body as if I'd been punched by a brawny senior. The simulator bridge—a model of the Federation's brilliant center of expansion, the brain of Starfleet. As I looked around at the buffed braces and efficient arrangement of control panels, Captain Kirk's words flowed back into my head . . . *And out there, everything's real.*

Commander Chekov led me down to the center deck, where the command chair stood in calm repose, facing the wide main screen.

I touched the chair's black leather, and his eyes said *sit down*, but . . . I couldn't. I just couldn't.

There were already other people here. Four . . . five.

Chekov nodded at the upper deck, where Sturek, formerly the Vulcan terrorist, stood enraptured by the science station, very focused.

"That is Cadet Sturek, your science officer," he said quietly, pointing.

"Yes, sir," I told him. "It threw me when he came in shooting during the ceremony. I've never even seen him swat a fly before."

"Mmm." The commander didn't seem impressed by the fact that I was impressed. His thick Russian accent added a certain finality to his cryptic promise. "I hope you like each other, because you'll be together for a long time. Over there is Geoffrey Corin." He pointed at the black cadet, the same guy I'd smooshed into the stage deck. Now he was standing on a stool with his head in the bridge rafters, doing something to the lighting. "Your navigator," Chekov finished. "He comes from a wealthy family on Alpha Centauri."

"Alpha Centauri? But he looks human."

"He is. The Federation has had a colony there for thirty-two years," the commander explained. "Didn't you know that?"

"No, sir, I guess I didn't."

"He has trouble taking Starfleet seriously." Chekov eyed Corin in a critical way. "He was up for command candidacy, but he didn't like the responsibility. He's here because he can shave days off a warp journey with navigation tricks. But there are risks to that kind of success. As team leader, you'll have to judge those risks."

My stomach twisted.

"Jana Akton, your helm officer," Chekov continued, nodding at the young human woman with the brassy blond hair tightly bound on top of her head, the same one who had led the way in from the auditorium wings. "She comes from Rigel Twelve mining colony in the Levintine Expanse. A rough place to grow up . . . even the weather is against you. She has a touch for subwarp piloting, but had some trouble with the technicals. That also will be where you come in."

Was he enjoying doing that to me?

Chekov turned to the command station, where Robin already had panels off and circuits exposed. "Your engineer, Robin Brady, you also know."

"Yes, sir. We're roommates."

"Not anymore. Now, as leader, you'll have your own cabin. Privilege of command. How Brady learned to rip and patch warp drive out on the *Rio Grande,* I've no idea. We chose him for his ability, but also because you know him and we feel it's good to have someone you know on your team."

He leaned one elbow on the command chair—I couldn't imagine doing that—and nodded at the Andorian woman. Her blue skin and ice-white hair caught the cast of the ceiling lights. She seemed almost to be made of dust, standing there at communications, playing the board testily, avoiding the others with aloof superiority.

"Your communications officer is Vanda M'Giia," Chekov said. "Daughter of a prominent Andorian diplomat. That means upper-upper class on Andor, in case you don't know that either."

He *was* doing it on purpose.

"I've never heard of an Andorian taking on a challenge like Starfleet," I said. "Hope she can handle it."

"If not," Chekov said, "it will be your duty to fire her."

Shifting nervously from one foot to the other, I lowered my voice. "I hoped to get a command someday, sir . . . but I sure didn't think it'd be on the first day."

"Well, it is."

His bluntness took me by surprise. I'd hoped for a comforting word of wisdom. Guess I wasn't going to get one.

"You're scheduled to fly your first simulator mission in about fifteen minutes," Chekov told me. "Make your first log entry, introduce yourself to your crew, and then will come your trial by fire. I hope you're ready for it."

He pushed off the command chair as if it were just an old couch and headed for the entrance with a swagger in his step that left me tense.

I touched the command chair's comm panel. "Cadet's log, first entry. Cadet David Forester logging on . . ."

Chapter 3

"Receiving over fifty distress calls . . . all garbled . . . there's tremendous interference in this whole sector—"

"Sensors are reading heavy impact residue and massive clouds of particle dust and warp exhaust."

"Does that mean there was a battle?"

"Very likely. If so, it was widespread and sudden."

Before us on the main screen, the hulks of dozens upon dozens of alien ships floated derelict. Or at least they appeared derelict. I didn't recognize the configuration at all. They weren't ships from any culture I was familiar with, and judging from the confusion on my crew's faces, they didn't know either.

"Did they fight one another?"

"Possibly," Sturek said, and adjusted his controls for more specifics. "However, all these ships are of the same general design, same interior pressure and life support systems, which leads me to conclude they are of the same race."

"So did we stumble on a civil war? Or should we search for attackers?"

He straightened and turned. "There are several options."

"How fresh are those readings, Sturek?" I asked. "When did this happen?"

"Spectral integrity indicates the residue is fresh within the past sixteen hours."

"Then this just happened. We're not looking at a graveyard or a scrap holding area. What's the—"

Behind Robin, the engineering console suddenly crackled, all the lights flashed, and half the screens went dark. Was the simulator broken?

No—couldn't assume that.

We'd been mapping the Golgotha solar system, sensor sweeping each planet and not finding much worth noting—which was my first clue that mapping wasn't the point of this mission. There wasn't much here, just gas giants, barren moons, and enough space dust to make the whole solar system look like a big cloud. If anybody could live on these planets, which they couldn't, they'd have a mighty ugly sky to look at.

Then we'd picked up an electromagnetic pulse that couldn't be natural, so we went looking for it. Now we were staring through the thick mud of space dust, faced with a field of more than fifty derelict ships whose design we didn't recognize.

So much for mapping. Who could lose fifty ships and not notice?

"Scan for life signs, Mr. Sturek," I ordered, puffing up a little. I took comfort in the protocol. One thing at a time, by the book.

"Scanning," he responded, and bent to his sensors.

"Do you want me to keep mapping, captain?" Jana asked.

I should've thought of that. "No, suspend mapping for now. Lieutenant Corin, move us in slowly. Ensign Akton, plot a course through the center of the field of ships so we can get perspective."

Wow—captain, lieutenant, ensign . . . sounded so strange to refer to each other by those ranks. We were nowhere near them, of course, in regular life. Maybe by the time we actually got there, they'd sound more right than they did here and now.

Jana turned and looked at me from her position at the nav console. "You want to just go right in there?"

Sturek was looking at me too. "That may be ill-advised."

"Why?" I asked.

"Whatever damaged these ships could be lurking nearby," he suggested.

"Or this could be a trap," Jana mentioned.

At the engineering console updeck, Robin added, "Or there could be high-intensity residue . . . y'know . . . harmful to our propulsion."

Damn, I hated good points. I *really* hated that I hadn't thought of those.

"All right. Sturek, scan the area for any other vessels that could be hiding in the system. M'Giia, try to identify the ones we can see. Jana, plot a loop around the field of ships and recon the solar system. Let's put on a sensor grid that'll selectively search for any ship movement other than what we can see. And let's catalog the derelicts—who should do that?"

M'Giia glanced at me. "I should do it."

"Okay, you do it. Corin, put the phaser banks on line."

"Phasers," Corin responded with annoying laziness, "on line, aye, oh, big chief."

"M'Giia, any identification on those ships?"

"No, sir, I'm not picking up any identifying signals, and the instruments don't recognize any emissions as familiar."

"Well, open a broad hailing frequency, then."

"You want to speak to all those ships at once?" she asked.

"As many as possible."

"Hailing frequency open, wide band."

Stalking the back of my command chair, I couldn't make myself sit down where the captain was supposed to sit. This wasn't exactly a shuttle's cockpit. Maybe after I killed a few invaders or arrested a few smugglers, I'd feel different.

Absurdly I cleared my throat before speaking. "This is Captain David Forester of the Starfleet science vessel *Agincourt*. We're picking up your distress signals and are ready to assist. Please identify yourselves and detail your damage and casualties."

What a dumb name for a ship. *Agincourt*. A medieval battle. What did that have to do with anything? Who made up these games anyway?

At the communications console, M'Giia listened to her earpiece and frowned. "Getting some kind of response, but . . . "

"Put it on the speaker."

"Aye, sir."

"*Grobbeiied thyoo shantto picniussh tou thenonsecu daiitaloo yosh clumus esthel ab eploiisin loofshoit comeesiver muut . . . *"

She clicked it off. "It's all like that."

"Universal translator?"

"On line and working. Something's garbling even the translation. When a universal translator can't make sense of what it's hearing, it reverts to the original language in case anyone speaks it."

Gripping the back of the command chair, I mumbled, "I don't speak that."

Evidently she didn't either.

"No communication," I muttered, trying to think. "By the book, what's next?"

"Scan for life signs," Sturek filled in, even though I hadn't really been fishing for an answer from any of them.

I glanced at him. "Do that."

"Scanning. Reading large numbers of low-level humanoid life signs . . . at least seventeen hundred. Picking up minimal but stable life support systems . . . and signs of repair attempts under way—"

"Repair? You mean they're trying to—"

PFFFOOM! A huge vomit of blue fire erupted from the propulsion stream of one of the nearby ships. We saw it, and two seconds later, we felt it.

Wave after wave of hard hits rocked the bridge—
that didn't feel like any simulation!

The helm fritzed and argued, and Corin raised his
hands away from the sparking board and didn't even
try to control the surges through his controls.

"Lock those down, Corin!" I shouted over the
boom boom of impact force.

He tossed me a disapproving shrug. "I'm not touching that! I'll get my fingers burned."

"Oh, poor you!" Jana leaned across the helm to
Corin's side and tapped off the power to the snapping
circuits, at least enough that the rest of the board
could be handled.

"Amazon," Corin chided.

"What's happening?" I called. "Are we under attack? Scan for hostile ships."

Boom boom—

"Reading no additional vessels," Sturek reported.

"Then what's causing that eruption?"

He worked his board briefly, then frowned. "Eruptions are tracing back to the pockets of space dust."
He spoke slowly as he did the analysis. The sensors
cast a soft jewel-toned glow on his face. "The phe-
nomenon seems to be toxic, reacting with the drive
sequences of these alien ships. The nearest alien ship
attempted to start its engines, and their method of
drive is reacting with the chemical construction of the
dust in this solar system."

"You mean their own drive is blowing them up?
That's what caused damage to this whole fleet? What
about our drive?"

27

"No adverse reaction to impulse exhaust, David," Robin reported.

"Their exhaust sequences read markedly more rich than ours," Sturek confirmed, and looked at me. "I believe we are safe to maneuver on impulse drive."

Another surge of energy blasted across us, and I lost my grip on the chair and ended up on one knee next to Jana.

I shoved myself back up. "Sturek, are you sure?"

"Negative," he said. "It's simply a conclusion based upon—"

"Good enough for me. M'Giia, keep trying to explain to them that we're here to help."

Another hit rocked the bridge, but this one was different, harder, shorter, and blew half of Robin's engineering console into a flashing mess.

I swung around. "What was that?"

"They're firing on us!" Robin called. He stood several steps away from his board, fumbling and unsure about what do to. "Why would they do that?"

"Maybe they think *we* fired on *them*," Jana said.

"That would mean they don't know what caused their damage," I concluded. "They don't know their own drive is doing it. M'Giia—"

"I'm trying," M'Giia insisted. "There's no way to break the garbling."

"Try the interstellar friendship code."

"I already tried."

"They're firing again!" Jana shouted.

I whirled toward the helm. "Corin, evasive action!"

"If you say so." He shrugged and picked at his board.

The shot got through before we moved an inch.

"Reading attempts at repair from at least thirty ships," Sturek informed us. "If they fire their propulsion systems, the entire solar system could become one large incendiary bomb."

"Understood." I coughed on the haze of smoke descending from the ceiling. "Robin, how many of those ships can we tow at once?"

"Four or five, I think."

"Don't think! Figure it out! Is it four, or is it five?"

Precious seconds were eaten up as he checked his systems. "It's . . . four."

"Jana, pick four ships and get tractor beams on. If we can pull them out of this space, they'll be able to use their engines without killing themselves. Then maybe they'll get the idea—"

"Two more ships shooting at us!" Sturek called over the crackle of damage, and a second later the ceiling exploded.

Chunks of bracing and conduit shell fragments from above and entire transfer cables came slithering to the deck, hot and sparking.

"Get those ships under tow!" I called.

"Tractor beams are on," Corin said. "What more do you want?"

On the upper deck, M'Giia twisted around in her seat. "They don't understand that we're trying to help them."

"I wonder why their weapons don't ignite the dust," I muttered.

"Better find out," Jana said, looking at her board, "because we're starting to score casualties."

I was losing crew. My legs started shaking. Emotions were getting the better of me—I could feel the creeping fear. "Astern, one quarter impulse, Corin!"

"Got it, quarter impulse, backing up."

"Just repeat the order!"

"Yeah, yeah."

"They're resisting our traction," Robin said. "They're powering up to fire again."

"And some of the other ships," Sturek rasped through the thickening smoke, "seem to be on a power build-up to fire on us also."

"How can I make them understand?" I paced between the helm and the command chair. "I don't want to shoot at them, but they're shooting at us . . . can we beam the survivors on board?"

"Seventeen hundred of them?" Jana shot back.

Robin said, "That much transporter power in quick succession would drain the impulse drive."

"I agree," Sturek added. "And the toxins in the space dust make transportation risky."

"Understood." I watched the ships on the screen, all just hovering and turning lazily in place. "M'Giia, hailing frequencies."

"We already tried—"

"Try again, please."

"Aye, sir, frequencies open."

"This is Captain Forester of the *Agincourt*. We are attempting to tow you out of the incendiary dust. Please cease fire. I could easily destroy you, but I'm not trying to! Cease fire! You are not under attack!"

"It won't work," Corin grumbled. "The program won't let it work."

"We can't treat this vessel like a program!" I derided.

"We're scoring damage," Jana said mournfully, "and more casualties. Now logging deaths in the engineering sections."

Frustrated, I shook my head. "All right, if that's the way it is. Corin, target one of the tow ships' weapons port."

"What?" He twisted around. "You want to fire on them after you said you wouldn't?"

"Right. Phasers at half power. Maybe they'll understand we're not trying to destroy them if we show them we can. Target their weapons port with a quick burst. Come on, do it!"

"Okay, if you say so."

"Give the correct response!"

"Okay, targeting, aye."

"Fire!"

The screen showed us our own phaser shot, lancing out through the murky brown globs of space dust toward one of the four ships we were towing. Red light swamped the alien ship's port aft quarter.

"Good hit," Corin reported.

"Hold your fire."

"Captain, that ship is powering up its propulsion systems!" Sturek called. "They're igniting engines!"

"M'Giia, broadcast interstellar cease and desist!"

"Broadcasting—"

Sturek spun around from his controls and threw up one hand almost as if to disengage himself from the bridge. "Too late!"

A blue plume boiled from the ship we'd targeted as

it fired its engines and tried to pull out of our tractor beam, and the pockets of space dust around us started to pop with ignition, blowing like fireworks between the four ships we had under tow.

"Break and run!"

"We can't leave them!" M'Giia called.

I watched the chain reaction erupting across the screen. "We can't stay! Send a call to Starfleet Command for backup!"

"David, the shields!" Sturek dodged back to his console.

How could I forget something like that!

"Full shields!" I ordered, but he was already putting them up, and it was already too late.

The blue-white eruptions ran along the stranded ships like the lines in a connect-the-dots puzzle, cracking open hulls and igniting exhaust and fuel as if the energy out there were hungry and hunting. On the screen, a sweeping hand of blue fire rushed through the pockets of exploding dust on its way toward us.

"Corin, vector us out of here! Full impulse!"

The blue wave surged toward us and overtook us, swallowing up my last words in a crackle of damage. The lights flashed, the ceiling snapped and sparked, and the consoles smoked. Warning signals flashed frantically and klaxons whooped, calling for abandon ship, but I couldn't make myself say that.

Just when I'd have had no choice if this had been a real ship, the computer voice boomed in my ears:

"Program shut-down. Your ship is destroyed. You sustained loss of all hands. Scores will be posted at sixteen hundred hours."

And all the sounds whined their last, then settled to silence. Even the normal bridge noises turned off. The sense of failure was complete.

I waved at the acrid smoke. "Well, I think we can agree that could've been better. Any suggestions?"

"Yellow alert might've been a good idea at some point," Jana droned.

That one made me wince. I'd completely forgotten the alerts.

Man, did my eyes hurt. This simulator was devilishly real, and my muscles ached for real too. My head felt like a balloon, my arms like iron.

"All right," I said with a sigh, "let's start cleaning up so the next team doesn't realize how badly we botched the program."

"What?" Geoff Corin swung around in the navigation seat. "Who's that! Oh, is that our captain speaking? Why, hello, Captain! Why don't *you* try steering a ship through something like that. I'd like to see how much better you'd do."

I tilted my head. "Don't eat your heart out, Corin. It's just a simulation."

"So was the opening ceremony," he reminded me wryly. "I think you busted my shoulder while you weren't taking it 'seriously.'"

I glowered at him, because that was kind of unfair, but if I told him it was unfair he'd think I was a wimp for whining. So I kept my mouth shut while M'Giia, Robin, and Jana Akton arranged a couple of stools and climbed up to the ceiling conduits, which were sparking all over me and Corin. I stood up and started handing them tools and receiving parts and panels from them.

"He thinks he's a commander because James Kirk took a shine to him," Jana said, sweeping me with her cold glare. "I say he just got lucky."

Robin stuck his head out of the ceiling. "Lucky!"

Everybody looked at him and he shut up suddenly, unable to muster any more defense.

"Cadet Forester deserves credit," Sturek said fluidly. "He was the only one who took action." As I cast a grateful glance up there, he frigidly added, "Even though it was non-regulation action."

Oh, fine.

Robin handed me down a cable, and I attached the end of it into a circuit trunk on the deck. The simulator was a wreck. Now we had to clean it up for the next cadet team. Minutes to decimate, hours to mend.

"I didn't think about regulations," I said. "I just reacted. I'd say Corin's right. I got lucky. Captain Kirk thought my action was right for the moment, but I could just as easily have gotten everybody killed."

"Don't throw me no bones, man," Corin said.

I turned to him and fanned my arms. "What—I can't be a *humble* tyrant?"

They all stopped and stared at me. Then Corin, amazingly, cracked a smile. Jana's stance eased off some. M'Giia glanced at Sturek, then back at me. All hands relaxed a little—I wasn't imagining it, was I? Had I actually gotten them to move over to my side a little bit?

Corin made peace by taking a tool I was holding

and passing it up to Robin. Jana stepped up onto one of the stools and braced a chunk of dangling hardware while M'Giia worked on the loose piece, and a small funnel of sparks shot down onto me and Corin. We both ducked, and almost bumped heads.

"Luck is nice," Jana said, "but I wouldn't depend on it. I never have."

"I don't consider luck," M'Giia offered. "I joined Starfleet because I have something to offer. Andorian society offered me only luxury as a lord's wife. I want to make my own decisions."

More sparks fritzed from the ceiling, and we all ducked.

"Procedures aren't perfect," Jana went on crustily once the sparks died. "Neither is Starfleet."

"Neither are we," I mentioned.

"Speak for yourself, Benevolent One," Corin drawled.

Jana leered down at him. "What got a clown like you into Starfleet, Corin?"

"My parents," he said as if he'd heard that question before. "They bought me the best schools, the best teachers, the best clothes, and Starfleet."

Jana's face cranked into a terrible grimace. "Starfleet isn't for sale!"

"I dunno," Corin snapped back. "I got a great deal on a shuttlecraft—"

Jana's cheeks flushed with anger. "Starfleet may be a joke to you, but I worked my way out of the mines to get here!"

The stool tipped under her and she almost dropped the mechanism she was holding up.

"Jana, don't drop that!" M'Giia warned.

"Lookee, folks!" Corin crowed. "We got us a super-charged holedigger right here at the Fleet! Should we genuflect or what?"

"You dirty show-off punk!" Jana plunged off the stool, and would've dropped the mechanism if Sturek hadn't plunged in to catch it, but that only stopped it from landing on my head. It didn't stop the connections from snapping.

Hot sparks and arcing electricity skittered from the ceiling as if Jana were some kind of comet and those were her tail. She got Corin by the collar and rammed him backward. They crashed into the command chair and rolled from there to the lower deck.

"Jana!" I grabbed her by the arm. "Back off!"

She twisted around. "What? Me?"

"A little innocent ribbing and she can't take it," Corin grunted from the deck.

Jana took a swipe at him. "You insulted me and I don't have to take it!"

"No, but you can't threaten a fellow cadet," I said. "Corin, apologize."

"David, *she* jumped *me*!" Corin wailed.

"Apologize," I insisted, "or you'll deal with me instead of her."

Big threat. Jana could probably bench-press me and Sturek at the same time.

But what the hell, it sounded good, didn't it?

Corin got to his feet. He took a step back and looked at Jana. "Sorry. Okay?"

"I guess," Jana huffed.

Beside me, Sturek held the manifold and seemed to

be inwardly grinning, if that was possible. I never thought it was until now.

Robin Brady glanced from cadet to cadet, wondering if the moment of surrender might explode into another fight, as if we weren't bruised enough for one day.

One day . . . all this on the first day of command school. What next?

"Nice smooth beginning," I sighed. "I can't wait till things get rough."

"Good afternoon, crew."

I strolled into the cadet lounge, hoping my tone of pseudo-pretentiousness would lighten the mood.

"I asked you all to meet me here so we could all get acquainted in something other than a hail of sparks. Did everyone get a drink?"

Corin held up a glass of something brandyish. "Any chance of something stronger?"

"Not on my salary." I took a seat between Robin and Jana Akton, noticing that Jana and Corin were sitting about as far apart as they could manage in the clutch of lounge chairs. On the other side of Jana, M'Giia sat even more rigidly than Sturek, who was actually more relaxed than any of them. Well, except Corin. He evidently had relaxation down pat.

"So what did you think of Captain Kirk's speech this morning?"

"I think he's dead right," Corin said. "We're sure not the best of the best."

"Well, he's got *something* right," Jana countered.

"He's saved the Federation a dozen times. Mostly by breaking regulations."

"Or by backing up the regulations," M'Giia added. "He couldn't have been *that* much of a maverick and avoided court martial. He must've had something more on his side."

"Sure," Corin said. "He had the newness of the unexplored galaxy. He was out there working where there weren't any regulations, or where he had to make up new ones. He had it easy."

"Easy?" I skewered him with a look of complete bafflement. What an attitude!

M'Giia shook her head disapprovingly. "I don't like the idea of looking for ways to go against Starfleet regulations, even if James Kirk got famous that way. You can't invent a new rule for every situation."

"Statistically speaking," Sturek offered, "the current Starfleet regulations have brought the Federation unprecedented success."

"*We* don't have the choice to make," M'Giia said. "We're not James Kirk. If we don't follow established procedures, we invite chaos."

"Starfleet's not perfect," Corin told her. "And neither are regulations. I say we break 'em all."

"How did this come up?" I moaned. "I just wanted to get acquainted! Can we scroll back and start over?"

But Jana scowled at Corin and said, "Look, I didn't join Starfleet because I thought I knew better than the best minds in the Federation."

"Maybe you didn't," M'Giia interrupted, "but I know I have something to offer to Starfleet."

Snatching at a chance to change the subject, I turned to my right. "How did you get into Starfleet, Corin?"

"Bought my way in," he said around a sip of his drink.

Rats—I forgot about that sore point.

"This may be a joke to you, Corin," Jana shot, "but it isn't to me!"

"How'd you get here anyway, Jana?" Corin returned. "Stealing the ore shuttle or just hitching a ride on a barge?"

Jana braced against her chair. "Wing slug!"

"Down!" I put my hand out between them and risked having it bitten off. "Down, down. Both of you, stop."

Corin shrugged. "Well, if she can't take a joke—"

"You're out of line," I told him. With a glance at Jana I added, "Both of you are. Nobody acts like this on my crew."

"Oh, *your* crew." Corin slumped deeper into his chair.

I shook my head, despairing. "Look, maybe that's enough getting acquainted for today."

When I stood up, they all did. Apparently they didn't want to spend time together unless ordered to do so—not a good sign.

"Hi, Robin."

The voice, a woman's voice, startled me because I hadn't thought there was anyone else nearby,

"Faith . . . " Robin turned and turned into even more a tower of gelatin than usual.

The female cadet was pretty—pretty? She was practically a ballerina! For the first second I inwardly chided Robin for blushing, then noticed I was probably doing the same. *That* was an attractive girl!

"Can I talk to you for a minute?" The girl took Robin's hand—just like that!—as if they were going for a walk on a hillside.

Without introducing her, Robin glanced at me with a flicker of pure fear and kidlike infatuation, and let himself be drawn away by the siren.

"Mmmmm . . . " Corin spoke for the rest of us as we watched them go.

We stood there for a few moments, then I sighed and sat down again. We couldn't just stand and watch, could we? On the other hand, we couldn't file past them, gawking like fourth graders either. Sit.

Something happened then that took me by surprise. All the others sat down too. They were taking my lead. Was this what it meant to be in command? Not so hard.

We sipped our drinks, but nobody could muster small talk, at least not in time to make the exchange seem natural. The glances from Robin and—what was her name?—told us they were both aware we were *not* looking at them. She spoke, he shrugged, she shook her head, he shrugged again, she smiled. It went like that.

Corin put his drink up to his mouth and mumbled into the glass. "Mmfff ee want wiffim?"

"Mmm dunno," I muttered back, rubbing my nose to hide the sound.

"Didn't think," Jana murmured, trying not to be

obviously murmuring, "he was the type . . . girls go for."

Corin pulled his glass back from his lips and blurted, "What would *you* know about what *girls* want!"

Robin and the female cadet looked at us suddenly, and Robin turned four shades of miserable.

Seemed like a long time, but there she went, and here he came.

"Everything okay?" Corin asked him as Robin sat down.

"Hmm?" Robin's head snapped up, then almost as quickly went down again. "Oh . . . yes. Fine."

"We have all spoken," Sturek said then, "except Robin. In the interest of completeness, I suggest we hear from him."

Had I snubbed Robin without even realizing it? And was I being scolded for emotional abandonment by a Vulcan? Perfect. My personal log was going to read like a surrender.

"Robin?" I turned to him. "Have I been ignoring you?"

"Oh . . . uh, no, no." He seemed as out of place as any cowboy might be here in this pleat-perfect place. That's what he was, after all, a Colorado loner who happened to have a touch with warp engineering. Maybe that was lucky, or maybe it was bad luck. I'd never been sure. Until lately he'd been my roommate at the Academy and pretty much hidden behind me, but those days were passed. He was on a command training team now. I wouldn't be able to protect him anymore.

But he wasn't one for talking to girls. So what had that cadet wanted with him?

We could all tell what he saw in her, though. I didn't know detail for detail what made some girls magnetic, but whatever mad scientist had built that cadet sure knew the formula.

With a certain look I reserved for times like these, I egged him on under the skewering gazes of our new teammates.

"I wasn't . . . sure I wanted to join Starfleet," he admitted, his voice getting fainter by the word. "I was happy working on the weather control satellite thruster systems, but Starfleet's a lot more . . . " He almost hit a stride, then looked at the carpet. "I don't need to talk, really."

"A lot more what, Robin?" I encouraged.

He raised his eyes and blinked as if I'd slapped him. "A lot more socially . . . complex."

"Socially complex!" Corin howled. "Hah!"

I swung around and snapped, "Corin!"

Corin deflated like a balloon and cuffed Robin on the arm. "Sorry."

Robin's face turned pink and he looked down again. His voice dissolved to nearly nothing. "I just wanted to serve . . . that's all."

"I concur," Sturek said amiably. "When one has capabilities that are of use to many, service is a logical response."

"I agree," M'Giia offered.

Jana nodded. "Absolutely."

"And we'll all get that chance," I said. Picking up my glass, I added, "To the crew."

Sturek raised his drink, and so did the others. "To the crew," he said.

And we all looked at each other, and I wondered how long the promise would hold.

"Once you're out of direct communication with Starfleet, you'll face challenges we cannot anticipate. You think you understand the distances, but you don't. And despite the events presented in the first two simulations, we are *not* just testing your combat ability. You must be able to make well-informed decisions on your own."

Captain Sulu was lecturing, and behind him Commander Chekov demonstrated the same piloting sequence as we'd just run in the simulator, this time running the dangerous pattern on a small simulator screen in the briefing room instead of the big one on the mock bridge that we had so effectively turned to rubbish.

Chekov was doing all right, but asteroids and space debris "hit" his "ship" from time to time, making lights and sirens flash and whine. Several cadets were watching, most of whom I didn't know yet. I was glad to have Sturek standing beside me. We didn't know each other well, but in this new environment, even one familiar face helped.

Smiling at Chekov's difficulties, Sulu said, "We train you on simulators, but believe me, the open galaxy is no simulation. Your crew will have to live with what you decide. For instance, Commander Chekov here would've been dead several times already."

Chekov struggled with the controls, but twisted around and gasped, "This has been upgraded! Why didn't you tell me! I should make you show them!"

"Big talk from a dead man," Sulu drawled.

Boom—the simulation on the screen showed a pulverized ship and Commander Chekov actually winced as he pushed himself away from the controls. "That's it! I'm dead! What kind of lesson is that?"

"It's the next great Russian tall tale."

Chekov pointed at him and said, "Only in Japan!"

"Maybe. But I'm from San Francisco." Captain Sulu folded his arms and broke out in a triumphant grin.

"All right . . . all right, shut down! Shut it down! Corin!"

"I'm doing it!"

"Use protocol! Say 'aye'!"

"Aye aye, sir!"

Jana cast me a glance. "Are we getting a little full of ourselves?"

Blistered with spark burns and still shedding hot matter from my arms and shoulders, I dragged the back of my hand across my wet forehead and ignored her.

The simulator was a wreck again. State-of-the-art technology had whipped us a second time. The best and brightest were dead. Again.

"Oh, sure," I moaned.

Behind me, Robin coughed. To my right, M'Giia spat a bit of insulation off her lower lip. Corin shook his hand, which was reddened from some stray electrical snap on the helm console.

"Why don't they build more safeties into this thing?" he complained.

Jana stepped around the helm past him and scooped up a length of cable. "What good would that do?"

She piled the cable back into its trunk, which had been blasted open by the enemy attack we had allowed to cut through to us. I felt as if she were stuffing my innards back into my gut, and they didn't quite fit anymore.

By the time we put the simulator back together, cleaned up, scrubbed the walls of all the soot and buffed out the scratches, my whole body ached and all I wanted to do was get back to my quarters. I wanted to lie down, sleep, snore, do inactive brainless things like breathe and twitch.

There was no sympathy in the known universe. I had to review the mission. I had to figure out how to avoid doing a third time what we had done twice already. If I'd been the only one at risk, that bunk over there would've sucked me in like a giant flange, but unfortunately Mr. Jump-on-the-Platform was now team leader and I had five other people depending on me.

While I watched our march to destruction for the fifth time and the mission shots became a lovely blur before my eyes on the desk screen, the door chime sounded and almost severed every nerve still working in my spinal column.

"Come in." Did I sound at least humanoid?

The door opened, and Jana stalked in. Her lips were set, her hands clenched, and her shoulders tight.

Well, at least one of us was awake.

"Is this a bad time?" she asked, but her posture told me she wasn't leaving, bad or good.

"Hi, Jana," I croaked, then cleared my throat. "Have a seat. What's up?"

"It's about Corin," she said bluntly. "He's out of control! He's not pulling his weight. He's a spoiled brat."

My head rattled when I nodded. "If I didn't know better, I'd say you didn't like Corin."

"Oh, no, I'm secretly in love with him. That's why he drives me crazy. He's the weak link in our team. We get evaluated as a *team*. He'll drag us all down. A *real* commander would think that was a problem. This is going to determine whether we get assigned to a starship or a garbage scow!"

"You're right," I said, still stuck back on that "real commander" crack. "We should get rid of him."

Pausing, Jana blinked, squinted, and shook her head. "What?"

Taking the moment to stretch my back muscles, I let her off the hook. "Okay . . . look, I understand, but we're all new at this."

She frowned. "It's affecting Robin too. Haven't you noticed how he's been in the simulator?"

Too exhausted to put A plus B together myself, I drew a sustaining breath. "How's Corin's attitude affecting Robin?"

"Haven't you noticed how he's been acting in the simulator?"

I blinked. "Which one? Corin or Robin?"

"Robin! *And* Corin!"

Her expression made me scared to ask again.

After a moment of grilling silence from me, Jana sighed hard. "Look, it's not that I mind Corin's going out with that cadet. It's just that he wasn't even interested in her until he found out that Robin had a crush on her."

Was the room spinning? "Hold on—you lost me. What cadet?"

"I'm talking about Faith Gage. Haven't you heard about this?"

"I've been busy."

Evidently I was expected to monitor the love lives of my crew. Or maybe Jana's hair was pulled back too tight.

After a moment I asked, "Is this that same girl who was in the lounge today?"

She held out a hand. "Yes, of course! This is serious!"

"I don't know, Jana," I protested. "My crew's personal lives don't really fall inside my command sphere."

"When we wash out, you'll change your mind."

"Okay, okay, you're right about that. I'll talk to Robin and see what's up. Next mission, investigate my crew's love life and see if it's compromising our survival. I'm starting to see that garbage scow in my future."

Jana's hard eyes eased some. She seemed satisfied—at least, as satisfied as Jana Akton could get. "Don't tell him I talked to you," she added.

"I won't."

"Are you ready to go?"

"Go? Where should I go?"

"Back to the simulator."

"We just got off the simulator an hour ago!"

"What about the Old Soldiers Mission? Didn't you look at Captain Sulu's all-hands memo? We've been moved up because of demand for use of the bridge simulator. Our results are due at zero eight-thirty."

"Jana?"

"Yes?"

"Would you kill me now, please?"

Chapter 4

"He thought it was a miracle, but I said it couldn't have been God, because God was commanding the *Enterprise* at the time!"

"That was your own fault."

"My fault? *My* fault? Those were real attackers, not simulations, which is all you had ever seen before that. And you didn't mind steering the *Enterprise* where I told you to that day. And all the days before, and after."

"I was carrying you."

"Carrying? How many planets would have had to jump out of your way without my navigating?"

Had I come in at the wrong moment? The two voices were strong and laced with underlying enthusiasm. The simulator was fritzing and smoking, real debris from a fake battle, and Captain Sulu and Commander Chekov were waving away the smoke.

Had they been using the simulator? Two senior officers, playing on the simulator?

I turned to leave—quickly, but Sulu called, "Forester! Front and center."

"Sir!" Turning on a heel, I came to attention on the upper deck.

"You tell us. In Simulation 4-A, should you go to Scenario Z or Scenario A?"

The two officers stared at me. Was there a right answer?

So I told him what my team had done. "Uh . . . scenario Z—"

"Not you too!" Commander Chekov blurted.

Oh, right. We'd botched that simulation.

"Or scenario A could work," I filled in quickly.

"Great minds think alike," Sulu said, grinning devilishly. "After all, this was the boy who clipped Captain Kirk, remember?"

"I remember!" Chekov snapped. "You two are ganging up on me. I'm going to put a demerit in Forester's file."

"Right next to the commendations I'm giving him." Sulu smiled again, this time at me.

Now I could actually smell the garbage scow. "Permission to go hang myself, sir?"

"You stay right here," Sulu said. "You can help Commander Chekov with his neurofeedback resolution reprogramming. Is that your report on the team's results?"

"Oh . . . yes, sir."

"Good. I'll go have a look." With one final victorious grin at Chekov, Captain Sulu vectored into the fake turbolift and left the two of us alone on the simulator bridge.

"You know," Chekov said, eying me, "I've known Captain Kirk since I was twenty-two . . . and *I* never got to hit him."

Agony.

The "lift" doors parted and for a horrible instant I thought Captain Sulu was returning, but instead a burly cadet strode in, the same senior who'd threatened Robin in the auditorium. So it hadn't been a trick of the prism sunlight—he really did have more muscles than I'd seen on most draft horses.

"You Forester?" this guy asked bluntly.

He darned well knew who I was.

"Identify yourself, cadet," Commander Chekov interrupted.

The burly guy flinched, as if he hadn't noticed there was an officer present. How could he have missed seeing Chekov?

"Yes, sir! Cadet Frank Malan, sir, senior command candidate, sir."

How did anybody get that stiff in only a couple of decades?—but Chekov wasn't intimidated, in spite of his slight stature against the cadet's solid-rock frame.

"Report, Cadet Malan," Chekov allowed after a critical silence.

"Captain Sulu sent me in to inform Cadet Forester that his team is expected on the phys ed field in fifteen minutes, sir."

"Fifteen minutes?" I gasped. "Then that's been moved up too!"

"Yes," Chekov confirmed. "With a large incoming

cadet class this semester, we're having to adjust the schedule."

"Permission to gather my team, sir!" I was suddenly breathless as my mind shot into responsibility mode—how was I going to get the whole team on the soccer field in fifteen minutes? I didn't even know where they were.

"Granted," Chekov said. "But report to the science lab in the morning. You're going to learn about simulators from the inside as well as from the command chair."

"Aye, sir!"

I hadn't meant to yell, but that's the way it came out.

A rush through the Academy dorm complex gathered most of my crew and we made the fifteen—okay, sixteen—minutes. By the time we reached the soccer grounds, we were already winded and I, who had done the most running, was cursing the practice of not using our comm badges during off hours. Oh, we wore them, but we weren't supposed to use them unless an officer authorized emergency contact.

During my first year, I'd been annoyed by that practice, but gradually got the idea that it existed to make life harder on cadets. That was the whole idea of any military academy—harder, not easier.

Well, today . . .

The idea wasn't to play soccer, and we weren't. We were using soccer balls and kicks and twists and dives to improve our physical condition, in a relay between command teams. I'd been doing this kind of thing for two years already, of course, as part of the usual

Academy torture, but I was finding out that the senior command candidates were particularly brutal, and one of those turned out to be good old stonyfaced Frank Malan himself. He'd arrived on the field before I did, which made me plenty suspicious about just why he'd been the one to come get me off the simulator bridge.

After a half hour, I was stumbling.

I'd gathered the whole crew, except for Robin, who'd disappeared into the ethereal mist. On all these acres of training grounds and research facilities and simulation complexes, why was he out of touch with his command team?

Just as a fleeting fear struck me that Corin's attention to that girl might've shoved my shy ex-roommate off the deep end of the Bay cliffs, I veered into a textbook maneuver to get the ball away from one of Frank Malan's brawny team and the maneuver completely betrayed me. The textbook hadn't figured on Frank Malan.

He appeared out of the sun—just like those old World War One stories!—and met me halfway through my beautiful execution of a spin kick. His foot found my shin, crippled my spin, and I went down hard, buffeted only by the strong hot breeze off the Bay.

I rolled onto a bruised hip, grimacing, my whole leg gone numb. "Ow—"

Frank stumbled back a couple of steps and stared down at me, his melonlike biceps glistening under the California sun.

"That's what you get for perfection, plebe," he ground in.

Gathering one breath just so he wouldn't have the last word, I grumbled, "I'm not . . . a plebe."

He smiled. Why was he so pleased about that?

Turning away, he waved to his team and called them to gather up from the reaches of the field, where they were sparring with my crew.

As I lay there wincing, the Jefferson Rose Garden mockingly winked at me from the sparkling complex of Starfleet Command on the crest of the foothills, gazing down its traditions at me.

"Yeah, yeah," I moaned. "Shut up, would you?"

Malan's crewmates were closer than mine, so they got here first. Was this a pattern?

"You all saw that, right?" Malan said loudly, to his gathering command team. "This is what I mean. That's what you get for following regulations and being a good soldier. It's no way to survive. There's got to be more to command than regulations, or an android could go out and do it."

I tightened my burning muscles and forced myself to my feet before Jana, M'Giia, Corin, and Sturek could reach me. Wouldn't look good to have them all helping me get up. They drew up on either side of me, and they were all watching Malan as he pranced before his team. Did they admire him?

"You're right, Frank," M'Giia said, panting from her run. "The best captains make things up as they go."

"Especially Kirk," Corin offered. "He broke the

regs all the time. He was the only cadet ever to beat the Kobayashi Maru No-Win Scenario on the bridge simulator. I'd sure like to know how he did that one!"

Oh, great. Hero worship. Another fine hurdle I had to knock down—and for my own hero.

"He was also brought up on court-martial charges," Jana pointed out.

"And he came out of it just fine.

"But because of the court-martial," Sturek said, "he was demoted from admiral to captain. I do not believe within human culture that is considered to be 'just fine.'"

Geoff Corin turned to me. "David, when you're a captain, won't you want some flexibility?"

The eyes of my team and Frank Malan's collection of neo-gladiators locked on to me. Real answer, correct answer, appropriate answer, or admit this was all a mystery to me yet because command was a lurking unknown . . .

I cleared my throat. "That's what I'm in the Academy to learn."

Mm, not bad.

"You should be a diplomat, not a captain," M'Giia snapped before my brilliance could sink in. "Regulations like the Prime Directive are fine for the idealists in the Federation, but if Starfleet faces an overwhelming threat, then we need to do whatever's necessary."

The sun turned her crayon-blue skin to blistering azure and made her white hair almost impossible to look at without getting sore eyes.

"It'll be our duty to enforce Federation law," I insisted, sticking to what I'd been taught, hoping that, like protocol, it would buoy me up.

Corin actually laughed, but nothing was funny. "If carnivorous nomads from the depths of space attack you and start eating your neighbors, you won't stop to check regulations. You'll open fire. The only diplomacy I'd need is a phaser bank."

"Whatever's necessary." M'Giia nodded, managing to agree with Corin and with herself at the same time. She moved a step closer to Malan.

"M'Giia's absolutely right!" Malan crowed like a politician, swinging around to address our two teams and the handful of strays who had come over to see what was happening. "The Federation expends too much of our resources coddling all these uncivilized races!"

I blinked. Had he just changed the subject? What was this all about?

"What?" I muttered. Raising my voice, I asked, "What??"

Malan swung to me. "Forester, these other races don't value the same things we do. They don't deserve the tolerance the Federation shows them."

Pushing between Sturek and Corin, I faced him. "Just what 'races' are you talking about, Malan?"

"The Klingons, the Romulans—and everybody like them! Who else, junior? You been in a box for two years or what? They're aggressive and vicious, and they're hostile toward races like us, and here we are trying to keep the peace with them!"

"And it's caused us nothing but problems," M'Giia added fiercely. "If it hadn't been for the Organian Peace Treaty, we'd have seen the complete destruction of the Klingon Empire by now."

When had I lost complete control?

"Look, we got a couple of decades of peace and quiet out of that treaty. It gave us time to work some things out."

"Peace," Jana put in, "isn't just the absence of war. Peace is solving real problems."

Enthusiastically, M'Giia added, "Holding two sides apart doesn't solve anything. Before the Treaty, we were beating the Klingons. Without it, we could've finished the job!"

Getting the feeling I was holding something apart, I turned to her. "Why are you taking this so personally?"

Her face flushed almost purple. "When I was a child, I was stationed with my aunt and uncle and four cousins on Luren Prime. The Klingons staged a massacre there. Everybody I knew was slaughtered. Even the children. Four thousand seven hundred forty-two Andorians." Her voice lowered, and somehow became easier to hear, and took on a notable dry rasp. "I was the sole survivor."

God, that sun was hot. *Sole survivor.* What would that be like?

Everyone looked at her. After a few seconds, they all looked at me.

What could I say?

Shifting my feet, I met her accusing gaze. "The

massacre on Lursen Prime was *before* the Organian Peace Treaty. I understand what you're saying, but it doesn't apply to today."

"Today," Malan broke in, "the Klingons are on the rampage again."

"Well, we better start polishing our phasers," Corin said spicily. "You too, Frank. They could be here any minute! I'm so scared!"

"With your scores," Jana drawled, "I'd be scared too."

"Oh, a zinger! Ow!"

"Shut up." I pushed him back and faced Frank Malan again. "I don't know what bug you've got in your ears, but don't try to incite my crew to violence. We've all got our hands full with the new training schedule, so let's just stay away from each other. Deal?"

"Oh, deal, deal," Frank mocked. "You can just tell the same thing to the Klingons when they show up. Deal?"

He motioned to his team, and they flocked away from us, encouraging other onlookers to break away too, and leaving my team standing in a sweaty clutch under the morning sun.

Casting a pathetic scolding glance at my biceps and wondering just why *they* couldn't do that, I noticed a movement in my periphery and lashed out with a quick hand.

Pulling Corin around from his attempt at escape, I asked, "Where do you think you're going? We have to talk about your simulator performance."

"Do we have to talk right now?" He glanced at the others.

"Yes, we have to talk right now."

He shrugged. "I know my sim scores aren't the best, but scores aren't everything, you know. Don't bother preaching. I know why I'm here. I'll concentrate harder. We've got our hands full."

"I know that," I said. "A command school curriculum is double the standard Academy work."

"I'm not failing," he insisted.

"Failing isn't the question. Your scores can bring down the whole team. Don't you get it?"

"Don't worry, Forester," he said with an edge. "I won't blow the team scores."

"Better not," I told him.

He bristled. "Don't lecture me, man. I'm not your puppy like Robin Brady."

There was more to say, but he was obviously embarrassed and that was tough for a guy like Corin to swallow. This wasn't productive.

So I decided to be unproductive in another direction.

"Speaking of Robin, any of you seen him?"

Jana huffed. "Have you checked about six feet behind Faith Gage? He's probably dogging her tracks and weeping."

"Come on. He's not *that* shy."

"He better be shy," Corin said, "if he gets between me and a woman I'm interested in."

Jana glanced at M'Giia, then back at Corin. "He probably can't run fast enough to get between you and any woman you're trying to chase."

"You'll never know, Rocky," Corin tossed back.

Well, this was slightly rotten. Handling a crew was harder than I thought. Why couldn't we just stick to rules and regs and say a lot of aye-sirs and do our jobs and that would be that?

They moved off, more and more space edging between them with every step. I lagged behind, watching their tense postures.

Behind me as I glanced, Frank Malan and his team strode off, laughing and clapping each other and roughing each other up as if they'd all come out of the same womb.

My team . . . the spaces were getting wider. The silence throbbed.

Would we ever be friends?

Should we be?

"Something veering out of the nebula's core— reading six renegade vessels on attack approach! Seven!"

"Red alert. Shields up."

"Shields, aye."

"Reading a rupture of shield stability! They're not holding!"

"Double power to the deflector grid. Drain the warp core if you have to, but get me some shields. Corin, port your helm, forty degrees Z-minus, one-half impulse."

"Renegade vessels are splitting up . . . four coming around to port—"

"They're heading us off! Corin, counter that maneuver! Robin, we've got to have shield power!"

"If I skim that much off the warp core, we won't be able to go to hyperlight."

"If you don't, we'll never get out of this nebula—"

Booom—fzzzzzz—crack

"That's it . . . shields are gone . . . "

"Thrusters off line. No more engine power."

"Program shut-down," came the amplified computer voice. "Your ship is surrounded by Venturi renegades. Your shields are down and you are out of power in a blanketing nebula. Scores will be posted at eleven-thirty hours."

"That's it. We've lost."

"Again." M'Giia bolstered Jana's comment with a glance of annoyance toward me.

"Time?" I asked.

Corin looked at his helm. "Took us exactly five point six minutes to get trapped like a fish in a net."

Beside him at the navigation console, Jana ran the numbers. "We held out sixteen seconds longer than the last time, but we lost ground in the maneuver."

"So we're ahead, but we're behind." I slumped in the command chair—yes, I'd finally made myself sit in it. After all, it was just a simulation. Just a fake. Pretend.

So why did I ache as if I'd been through the real thing?

Around us, the bridge was dusted with battle damage, fritzing and burping with sparks and smoke. Did a real starship ever get this beaten up?

"Not good," I said. "There's some combination of moves or decisions that gets us out of these situations. I just can't find them. And, Robin, you took way too

61

long to respond with those warp field shifts. Geoff, I've got to have quicker action from you too."

Waving at the smoke puffing from the "damaged" helm, Corin cranked around in his seat. "I can't make a move until you make a decision, boss."

"Look, I'm not letting myself out of the blame," I told him wearily, "but once I make the decision, your hands have to snap on the controls, or we slip. Dead's dead, after all. And 'boss' isn't the way you address your commanding officer."

"Oh, right," he droned. "Remind me when I get one."

Jana, Robin, and M'Giia looked around from what they were doing. Sturek was the only one who managed to keep his eyes on his controls, but I noticed his shoulders tense just a little.

Robin moved forward toward the rail, his lips parted as if he had something to say, and he fixed his eyes on Corin, but when Corin looked up at him, the lips clamped shut.

"Got something to say, lover boy?" Corin taunted. "Or did you just swallow a bug?"

The pain of embarrassment and crippling shyness crimped Robin's face. Whatever he'd had in his mind to say, he couldn't get it out. If he'd meant to defend me, or to finally challenge Corin about this girl they both had in their sights, the intent fizzled out.

"Okay," I said with a relenting sigh, "let's clean up this mess."

Not my most shining command moment. Academy protocol gave me the right to yell at Corin, at the very least to order respect out of him, but what good would that do? The respect was in the uniform, they told us, but there had to be more to it than that.

After all, Frank Malan was wearing a uniform.

No one looked at me as they spread across the deck, plucking up bits of cable and blown panels. Most of this stuff was meant to fall apart in some way or another, and we knew the engineers came in from time to time and redesigned the wrecker programs, but fake though it was we still had to clean it all up for the next team.

They weren't fooling anybody—all this blowup-cleanup process was to get us used to just how a ship's bridge was put together. By the time we got to a real starship, we'd know every little bolt, conduit, chip, and cell, because we'd have put every one into and out of place two hundred times.

Made me wonder what they did to train maintenance crews.

"Hey!"

"I don't need your help, Corin!"

"You sure don't! Anybody who wants to rush out and stir up trouble with the Klingons doesn't need help from me!"

"Then let go!"

Oh, not now—I swung around and found Corin and M'Giia playing tug of war with a fallen cable. On the upper deck, Robin had turned to stare at them, and even Sturek was looking this time.

One good yank from Corin wrested the cable from M'Giia's hands, which only seemed to anger her.

"I don't have to *start* trouble," she said. "The Klingons can get away with anything they like, as long as they leave no witnesses. Well, I'm a witness!"

"Hard to prove without evidence, M'Giia," Jana pointed out.

"Evidence?" M'Giia leaned over the helm console toward Jana. "What about facts? Who gains the most from breaking a treaty with the Federation! The Klingons! Who gains most from covering up their tracks! Klingons!"

"Again," Jana said, "no proof that the attack on Bicea was staged by Klingons."

M'Giia stepped back. "Maybe there's not, and maybe there is."

I stepped between them. "Are you saying you have proof, M'Giia?"

She leaned toward me. "I've heard Starfleet has sensor logs showing unknown ships in Federation space near the Klingon Neutral Zone. If it's not the Klingons, then who else could it be?"

On the science deck, Sturek moved to the bridge rail. "Circumstantial evidence," he pointed out. "Our surveys of that area are incomplete. What do you think, David?"

His question took me completely by surprise. In my experience, Vulcans weren't prone to ask much—just answer. Then again, wasn't that kind of parochial of me? Expecting people who looked alike to think and act alike?

With a crew of this makeup, I'd better quit that pronto.

Still, being asked to come to a conclusion by the

princes of conclusions—I felt the hot seat come up under me.

"Well," I began, "having sensor logs of unknown ships isn't what I'd call proof, but this morning Commander Chekov canceled our work on the simulator programming. He wouldn't say why."

"There could be plenty of reasons," Jana mentioned.

M'Giia nodded. "And war could be one of them."

"I never meant to imply that," I told her sharply. I was losing control again! "If there's trouble on the border, we'll find out soon enough. Starfleet Academy isn't exactly the first line of defense. Get back to work. The next command crew will be here in twenty minutes and this melt-down has to be put back together. Corin, just a minute."

As I tugged him aside, he protested, "Again? I told you, I'm doing my best!"

"I don't think so. You fumbled twice. You wasted seconds. We need those seconds. The team's only as fast as its slowest reaction. Right now, that's you."

Corin's dark face flushed with a touch of bronze, just enough to show me he was on the edge of blowing up. "We've been through this."

"And we'll go through it again until you deliver what you're capable of. I want you to study the maneuver protocols for three hours solid before our next mission."

Did I sound like a commander, or just bossy? What exactly was the difference? After two years in the Academy, I thought I knew, but now, standing at the delivering end instead of the receiving end . . .

Today only the uniform was keeping Corin from imploding my face. Sooner or later I had to get it right, with or without the uniform.

"Look," he began slowly, then sighed. "This stuff . . . it kind of scares me. I could always do it, but I never had to take a bunch of responsibility. This stuff about the whole crew's lives depending on me."

Feeling as if my skin was tightening, I had no idea what to say to that. He'd gotten through the courses and the training and the rigors of the Academy well enough to make command school—that meant somebody saw a potential senior officer in him, or at least in his talents.

Now this had landed on me.

I drew a breath, then talked without letting it out.

"What you mean is, you've been avoiding real challenges all your life, you've been protected by your parents' wealth, and you liked it that way. Don't you think it's time to walk the wire without a net?"

His eyes turned hot and his brows came down. "Why should I care what you think? I don't need the Academy. In fact, I don't need Starfleet. After all, I guess they got their fill of cowards."

"Hold it—" I caught his arm as he tried to step past me. We did an awkward dance over the spilled cables and ended up turned around, but I managed to keep him from walking away. "If you keep backing off, nothing'll ever improve."

"Improve?" Corin shook his head and lowered his voice, trying to keep this between us and the snapping sparks on the consoles. "And if I don't 'improve,' then everybody here is going to crash land? I don't mind being dangerous to myself, but when I get dangerous for everybody else, it's time to cut and run."

Maintaining my grip on his arm, I told him, "That's not acceptable and you know it."

"Oh, really? Well, tell you what, Captain Kid, what happens if I work harder and then mess up anyway? What then?"

"Then we'll be there to back you up," I said bluntly. "That's crew thinking."

As if I knew.

Buoyed by my promise—a whopper, by the way— Corin seemed surprised for a few moments. His expression moved through a half dozen emotions, including disbelief. Gradually he slumped out his belligerence, paused, then nodded and looked up at me. "You're going to see a big change."

He nodded again in agreement with himself and escaped to the upper deck, where he started helping Sturek reposition the sensor trunk housing.

Was that all it took? A couple of phrases of encouragement? Reassurance that we'd stand behind him if he botched a maneuver? Good for me. I'd have to try this more often. If only I believed a word of it.

"Cadet Forester, report to the commandant's office."

The comm voice almost unstitched my skin. I dropped the hot spanner in my hand and tripped on the cables.

"What do *they* want?" Corin straightened and looked at the ceiling as if it might answer.

67

"You know what they want," Jana said with a warning tone. "They monitor our performances console by console. Think they're stupid?"

"No, I only think *you're* stupid."

Jana laughed at his lame response. "Oh, bet that one took brainpower, Geoff."

For the first time since—when had I heard his voice last?—Sturek turned and spoke up. His voice had a clear edge of annoyance that made us all pay close attention.

"This is unconstructive," he said. "Such behavior risks our chances of succeeding as a command team. And I, for one, would rather not have on my record that my first command team fractured due to something as inefficiently visceral as personality clashes. Either fight with each other and be done with it, or decide not to. Make up your minds."

We all fell suddenly silent, with me wishing I'd said that.

Feeling that the wrong person had been made commander of this team, I shuffled up the bridge steps toward the turbolift.

"What're you going to tell them?" Corin asked.

M'Giia, Jana, Robin—they were all watching me.

I swept them with an unhappy gaze, which landed on Sturek's displeased glare.

"I don't know," I said. "Guess we'll find out."

Chapter 5

"Come on, Corin, support her foot! No one person can climb this!"

The athletic grounds were breezy and bright as we engaged in the Academy's idea of teamwork— working like dogs to climb a forty-foot tall artificial rock wall that nobody could climb alone. The whole thing was arranged that way—the only footholds and handholds were just at the right distance and stretch that we had to help each other at some point.

I'd made it to the top of the wall with Sturek's help, and below us Jana and Corin were struggling up, with Jana above.

Corin's brown face was pasted with sweat as he squinted up at me. "This is why civilized people invented transporters!"

"Come on, don't gripe!" I called. "We could've died five times already at this pace!"

"David!" M'Giia came jogging across the ground, calling for me.

"Up here!" I leaned over to get her attention, and darned near fell. Only Sturek grabbing me by the waistband averted a really embarrassing and painful moment, despite safety lines.

She shaded her eyes and squinted into the sunlight. "Commander Rotherot wants you to report to his office as soon as you finish on the field."

"Acknowledged. Tell him I'll be there. As soon as Corin gets his center of gravity up here. Come on, Corin!"

"It's just a drill, Forester. Our lives aren't really on the line."

"Wrong. If you don't step it up, I'll kill you."

"I expected better from you and your crew."

Wounds came from phasers, wounds came from knives, sparks, fists, but nobody ever told me that wounds came from senior officers.

Commandant Rotherot's simple sentence bruised me from my forehead to my anklebones. The sting of humiliation cut deep, but there was only one response a cadet could possibly make.

"Yes, sir. So did I."

Rotherot occupied himself with wiping up a dribble of what seemed to be tea, since that's what he was drinking, from the corner of his desk. "Despite your efforts, Corin's scores are still under par, and Engineer Brady's responses are less than innovative, and your communications officer seems distracted at best."

"Yes, sir. And, sir, in fairness I have to inform you that my own performance has been less than inspired."

"Really?" A deep voice sounded over by the couch.

Captain Sulu was leaning on the window brace, looking out over the athletic grounds where six squads of freshman cadets were running through midday drills.

"Command evades you, Cadet?" he went on when I didn't answer his non-question.

"It confuses me, sir," I admitted, anxious to vector the conversation off my team and onto myself. "But I'm aware of the problems, sir, and the team is pulling together to solve them."

"Be specific," Sulu instructed. "What kind of problems?"

My boots were suddenly tight. "Personality conflicts, sir."

Moving the neat stacks of papers on his desk to wipe under them, Rotherot paused suddenly and looked up. "Are you going to complain about personality conflicts when a Klingon heavy cruiser is barreling down on you? Do you know what you'll be up against? They've got a whole new—"

"Commandant," Sulu cut him off briskly.

Rotherot's beefy face flushed pink, and he almost seemed to have been punched. He stood there, half bent over his desk, holding the cloth he'd been using to clean in one hand and the stack of papers he'd moved in the other. And he stared at Sulu, then at me.

What was that about? What was there about

71

Klingon heavy cruisers that would make Sulu tell Rotherot to stop talking about them?

A chill ran down my back, swelling up a sensation of having been through this before. Something about this conversation was naggingly familiar . . .

"Sir," I began, and suddenly my throat seized up. I knew what I wanted to ask, but the actual business of asking turned my stomach upside down.

Sulu came around in front of me and sat on the corner of Rotherot's desk. Man, were they different from each other!

"Go ahead, Cadet," he prodded. "What is it?"

"Sir, how do I . . . replace a member of my crew?"

Oh—ow! God, where was the wastebasket! I had to throw up!

If only I even knew who I was talking about—Corin? M'Giia? Robin? Myself? Any minute now, Sturek and Jana would be filling all six bridge positions by themselves. Lot of jumping around.

"You don't," Sulu said sternly. "There's no changing crew in the middle of a mission. As Captain Kirk said, you do your best with the hand you're dealt. If your team isn't getting good results, it's up to you to tighten up their talents. Understood?"

No. Not a bit. Not a clue. Say it again.

"Yes, sir!"

"Dismissed."

I spun on a toe, and almost fell over a chair. Might as well. Couldn't look any more ridiculous than I already did.

The office seemed sixty feet long as I tried to get

out. My feet had turned to iron. The door panels sensed me coming and opened up—

And Vanda M'Giia stood there, escorted by a security guard. She looked confused, intimidated.

"M'Giia!" I spoke out. "What's wrong?"

"I don't know," she murmured. "They won't tell me."

"You're dismissed, Forester," Commandant Rotherot called from inside.

"Sir," I dared, turning, "if you're going to address a member of my crew—"

"This is personal, Mr. Forester," Captain Sulu said. "You're dismissed."

They didn't even wait for the aye-sir before shutting the door panels manually between M'Giia and me. The last I saw of her was the crimping of her shoulders as she faced two men she had never expected to speak to in person.

I could only stare at the closed gray panel, and listen as the servolocks hissed into place. It would take a phaser to get in there now.

The security guard took a position on the other side of the door panel, his posture communicating that I was finished here and really better move on. He didn't even look at me. Did he know what was going on?

I turned and forced myself to walk away, resisting the urge to set up camp ten feet outside the commandant's office. How could they talk to me about teamwork, then keep me in the dark about one of my teammates?

Outside the door of the building—the sun cut into

my eyes instantly and I paused for a moment to let them adjust, looking instead down at a squared boxwood hedge flanks by rows of coleus plants nodding in the offshore breeze. There weren't very many insects around because of the breeze, one of the little comforts that occasionally offset the physical duress of training. All we needed was flies and mosquitoes, right?

That sun really hurt. No, more than that—headache.

"Mr. Forester?"

I snapped to attention, expecting an officer or a senior, but found myself squinting at the female cadet who had come between Robin and Corin. Gage. Faith Gage.

"I'm Faith Gage. You wanted to see me?"

"Uh . . ."

"Jana Akton said you wanted to talk to me."

"Oh, she did . . . ah-huh. Well, I'm glad to meet the person who's been spending so much time with my crewmen."

"You mean Geoff Corin?"

I tipped my head. Just to test the water, I said, "Actually, I meant Robin Brady."

"Oh . . . Robin."

Bending my chin down to avoid the sun, I found myself staring at—parts of her an officer and gentlemen shouldn't stare at. So I faced the sunlight and tried to look at her hair or ears or—man, those were *some* eyes.

"Corin and I have a lot of fun together," she said. "As for Robin . . . I have him in a few engineering classes, and he's in my morning drill company, but he just can't get his head out of the Jeffries tubes."

"Well, he's pulled it out long enough to get downright infatuated with you," I mentioned honestly.

"Yeah . . . he's a nice kid, real tech-smart, but I couldn't be interested in somebody whose whole life is dilithium matrices. It's just not for me."

"I know. I've been trying to get him to do other things."

"Mmm," she uttered, nodding.

My eyes hurt, so I looked down again, and quickly up. Just couldn't slip like that. "Do you have any suggestions?"

She shrugged one shoulder, which did volcanic things to the places I was trying not to look. "Why doesn't he join one of the social groups on campus?"

I looked past her shoulder at the freshman barracks. There just wasn't anyplace on her that I could actually look.

"He's in a group on campus," I said. "He's in my crew."

She shrugged again—mmmm—and said, "Well, he needs some kind of outlet to break through all that shyness."

"I can't order him to be sociable. Maybe he'll listen to you, though. Could you make a little suggestion?"

Before she could answer, I noticed a movement past her shoulder—somebody was waving at me. And they were calling my name. Corin . . . Jana . . . Robin and Sturek, and a dozen or so other cadets.

They were running toward the activity center where the cadets' lounge was housed.

"David!" Jana called. "Commandant's about to make an announcement!"

"You'd better go," Faith Gage said. "I have to report to the foreign language lab."

She left without any other amenities, and I got the feeling she didn't want to be around Corin and Robin at the same time.

I broke into a run and met my crew at the lounge's inner doors, where Jana was just turning up the volume on the lounge viewscreen.

"Have you been watching the news?" she asked me, eyes wide.

"No. Why?"

"Rotherot's been repeating an announcement."

The screen cut in on the commandant in the middle of a sentence.

"—have been given official confirmation that the Federation colony on Bicea was destroyed two days ago by unknown forces. There are no survivors. First reports of this tragedy were made by the *U.S.S. Sentinel* at twenty-two-thirty last night—"

"Bicea," I murmured. "That's one of the main port colonies on the Klingon border, isn't it? How many—"

"Over two hundred thousand," Sturek filled in instantly.

Jana folded her arms around her ribs and seemed to ache.

Corin shook his head. "M'Giia had relatives there, David."

I looked at him. "Which relatives?"

"All the relatives she had left after Lursen Prime," Robin told me. "Her mother, four brothers—"

"Everybody," Jana choked. "The few remaining members of her family lived there. They were building a life in what they thought was a safe place. They were the primary Andorian ambassadorial link in the sector. Now they're all . . . "

Her last two words choked off and made no sound, yet we all heard them. *All dead.*

"Can she get some leave time?" Corin asked, as if he felt obliged to say something, to say anything.

Robin looked at me. "Bicea was one of the disputed planets along the Klingon Neutral Zone, wasn't it?"

"Yes," Sturek filled in when I couldn't speak up. "Treaty arbitration gave it to the Federation, but the Klingon Empire has never formally relinquished its claim. They never accepted the judgment."

The other cadets in the room were talking quietly also, and some listening to the words between us, or at least I got that feeling. Maybe I was just oversensitive, but they did know that one of my crewmates was from Bicea. They *seemed* to know, anyway, and that stayed with me. I felt all their eyes.

And I felt all their eyes shift—M'Giia was just entering the lounge.

Her blue complexion had gone storm gray. She didn't look around, didn't acknowledge anyone as she walked stiffly to us, not looking up at the screen where Rotherot was still speaking.

No one said anything. At first this struck me as cruel, when I abruptly realized they were all waiting for me to do the speaking.

This command stuff . . . there was too much to it.

"M'Giia," I began, tentative at best, "is there anything we can do?"

She raised her eyes to Rotherot's flat form on the screen. Strange how, set like jewels in the velvet field of her alien skin, her eyes could be so very human.

Her voice was frail, but filled the room as she shook her head very slowly.

"No one can help a sole survivor."

Chapter 6

"Robin—Robin, don't walk away."

"I think we should leave her alone."

"She doesn't want to be alone. Just let her sit there for a minute and talk to me. We're on the same team, but I hardly see you anymore. How did that happen?"

The cadet lounge was heavy, almost as if the air itself were filled with droplets of oil. Of the fifty or so cadets milling about here, watching Rotherot's repeated announcement or the airing of comments by various officials and media mouthpieces, no one could make himself be the first person to actually walk out the door and get about business of training.

Eventually, we all knew, training would come to get us. Our drill instructors, our lab instructors, our senior company commanders, or our brigade commanders would find us and we'd be pounding the field again, but for now our whole beings were caught up in the drama unfolding out on the Neutral Zone, almost as far out of our influence as Valhalla. We were only cadets. It was our job to care, yet not be able to lift a finger to help.

Someday . . . someday.

Confronting Robin had been something I dreaded, but now provided a distraction from dealing with M'Giia—which was a complete mystery to me. How could I comfort somebody whose whole family had died? I never even knew anybody who died before this.

How had I gotten to be over twenty years old and never had anybody close to me die?

Was I just that lucky? My parents, my uncles and aunts, cousins, all four grandparents, even two great-grandparents and two great-aunts—they were all still alive. Everyone I'd grown up with, gone to all those Christmas parties and summer picnics with . . . they were all still alive.

I glanced through the forest of cadet uniforms to where my crew were all sitting in one of the clutches of lounge chairs, with M'Giia in the middle. She was the only one whose face was unreadable. Even Sturek showed more emotion.

All right, concentrate.

"Robin, you've got to quit avoiding the rest of the crew."

His pale face and hurtful eyes told me what a moment later he spoke straight out. "They don't need me, David. I'm just the engineer."

"What kind of a sentence is that?" I demanded. "Did you hear what you just said? That's not acceptable or even true. With an attitude like that, you'll never make it through command school."

"Maybe I won't," he said, lowering his gaze to the carpet. "Maybe I'm just not cut out for the pressure."

"It's a little late for that," I pointed out. "We're in the boat now and we all have to row. Were you just going to avoid me too?"

"You've got the others now, David . . . "

"They're not 'others'! They're *us*!"

He wouldn't look up. "I can't fit in . . . I belong in a dark cave by myself. I should just go back to Colorado—"

"Robin, I don't get it. You've made it through two years of Starfleet Academy and been accepted to command school, and now suddenly you can't hack it? What changed?"

He raised his eyes without raising his chin, giving him a pathetic childlikeness, his expression filled with misery.

"You changed," he said softly.

Well, that wasn't exactly what I expected, was it?

"*I* changed? How did I change?"

"You got command, that's how." He looked into the carpet again. "We used to do everything together. We had the same classes, mostly. We had the same drill team. We had the same marksmanship company. We were in the same labs. Now, it's changed. You're my team commander. We can't even be roommates anymore. You don't even stay in the same barrack anymore."

I wanted to protest, to tell him he was wrong and reassure him that we could be the same barrack mates and lab mates and drill mates and target team we'd been for two years, but I knew he was right. The service was set up that way. Promotion had lead weights attached. One of the weights was that promoted officers weren't supposed to fraternize with junior cadets or those under one's command. There were reasons for that, I'd always known and understood, but I'd never been friends with a senior cadet or a commander before. Service fraternization protocol had never cost me anything before.

I parted my lips to tell Robin he was wrong, but he wasn't. Commanders had to be emotionally removed to some degree from their crews—otherwise, how could a leader be expected to send his best friends out to their deaths? And we all had to be ready for that. The distance had to be firmly established, or no one could stand the pain.

Military chain of command had been like this since the raw beginnings—a necessary coolness offset by loyalty to cause and active support. We weren't supposed to be a family. We were supposed to be a crew.

Robin knew that. I hated that he knew it and I couldn't fool him. I couldn't protect him anymore. His shyness was turning into a crippling illness. If I didn't shake him out of this, he could pay with his life, or with someone else's.

"You can merge your abilities with the others," I told him. "Leaders like James Kirk had great engineers behind them. Look at all the brilliant work Montgomery Scott and engineers like him have done in Starfleet. You want to know whether or not you can measure up to him, don't you?"

"That's not fair." He looked up sharply and started shaking. "This is easy for you. I just don't fit in!"

"Take it easy," I said. "I'm not trying to corner you. I want you on the team, not off it."

"I'll let you down."

"No, you won't."

"David, I'm grateful for your loyalty, but I just don't deserve it."

He tried to turn away, but I caught him. Exasperation came out in my voice. "Okay, let's do it the hard way, then. You *will* spend time with our team, you *will* try to communicate more, and you *will* quit talking this way. That's an order."

His face went pasty with hurt, but I couldn't help that. Neither of us had ever borne the responsibility we did today. The honor of command was going sour.

"It's all lies!"

I flinched at the clear bell of M'Giia's voice cutting through the solemn crowd of cadets.

She'd come to her feet, and was shouting at the big viewscreen.

On the big viewscreen was a big Klingon in a big robe—a Klingon high councilman.

"—no matter what the Federation claims. The Klingon Empire had nothing to do with the loss of the Bicea colony. However, there is bitter justice in the colony's failure. The Federation should never have put fragile Andorians and humans on such a hostile world. Only Klingons could have tamed Bicea."

"Liar!" M'Giia cried again.

One of the cadets near the viewscreen took that as a good reason to turn the volume down, and luckily the scene switched away from the Klingon councilman to somebody else.

"What about the energy readings from Bicea?" Geoff Corin said as Robin and I joined them. "Those were Klingon disruptors!"

"That does not prove Klingon involvement," Sturek pointed out evenly.

"Oh, I see! It was all those *other* races that live near the Klingon border and use disruptors!"

M'Giia turned to our Vulcan teammate. "Why are you making alibis for the Klingons, Sturek?"

"I regret your loss, M'Giia," he told her, "but Bicea was not a critical colony, nor was it strategically placed. It is illogical to assume that the Klingons would start a war over a world that would gain them nothing. We cannot blame one race when all facts are not known."

"Just like a Vulcan!"

Boy, had M'Giia's voice changed—

Nope—that was Frank Malan. Just what we needed.

He shouldered his way through the parting sea of cadets. "Just like a Vulcan to deny the obvious in search of details! Using logic to soften the truth. The Klingons should be destroyed for the monsters they are!"

A surge of agreement rose across the field of cadets. Encouraged by that, Malan swung around to face the crowd.

"The Federation should change its whole approach to Klingons!" he went on like a country preacher. "The treaty robbed us of the war we needed, and because of that the Klingons grew stronger! Now look!"

"Pretty strong words, Frank."

My eyes widened. What idiot had said that?

Oh . . . it was me.

His face was a plaster cast of rage as he swung around. "The attack on Bicea was an act of war. We can't let it go unpunished!" Dropping me like a stone, he swung back to the attentive crowd of infected cadets. "We need new leaders who aren't afraid of the Klingons! We need the Vanguard!"

The cadets cheered him. Frustration at our impotence in the galaxy's troubles drove them to approve of Malan's words.

"The races inside the Federation already live the right way. It's the races outside that're the problem."

"Vanguard?" Corin interrupted. "What's the Vanguard?"

"It's a political action group that has humanity's best interests at heart. They're as tired as we are of Starfleet's timid response to the Klingons. The Vanguard says it's time for humans to take care of humans!"

The cadets nodded again, but not quite with the same fervor as a moment ago.

Sturek voiced the reason. "And all the other Federation races?" he asked, his presence suddenly powerful here. "What will your Vanguard do with them?"

Malan looked at him, noticed M'Giia and the other non-human cadets—though admittedly there were very few—and backpedaled. "The races inside the Federation already live the right way. It's the Klingons and Romulans, that're the problem. The Vanguard calls for a sense of order in the galaxy. We want to make the Federation strong!"

I crossed among a half dozen cadets to challenge him. Well, somebody had to, right?

"We?" I asked. "I take it you're already a member of this group?"

Suddenly uneasy, Malan glared at me. "What if I were? You think I'd bother discussing it with you, junior? You'll remember my words someday."

Under the pats and nods of other stirred up cadets, he proudly turned away and was absorbed by his command crew and a clutch of others who liked what they heard.

I didn't blame them. I was frustrated too. But . . .

"Sounds frightening," Jana uttered, watching Malan leave.

In the middle of us, M'Giia watched Malan too. "Sounds fascinating," she countered. "They might be just what the Federation needs."

"Look!" someone called, and all eyes went to the big screen again.

On the black matte of space, with only a single lonely spider nebula winking in the upper left corner, a Federation starship veered across the top of the screen, dodging between two Klingon Birds-of-Prey and firing at both of them at once.

The crowd of cadets cheered mightily at the strike.

"Starfleet finally struck back!" Frank Malan crowed, one arm around his science officer and the other vaulted into the air over our heads.

A voice-over announcer spoke off the screen as we

watched the *Sentinel* take on the Birds-of-Prey. "—was recorded this morning by a passing tanker just this side of the Neutral Zone—"

"Who won?" I wondered aloud. "Come on, give!"

"There were no ships destroyed, no loss of life," the announcer continued obligingly, "but the Klingon attack ships were driven back across the Neutral Zone without fighting to the death. Federation spokespeople claim—"

"We finally struck back!" Malan boasted, his voice drowning out the announcer. "The captain of the *Sentinel* showed the Federation how a real starship captain acts!"

"The engagement ended inconclusively," Sturek corrected, apparently disturbed by Malan's editorializing.

"No one here knows what the captain acted like, Malan," I said. "Any chance for a speech, right?"

He twisted toward me. "What's the matter, Forester? Afraid you might actually have to go out and fight some day?"

"Are *you* afraid the facts won't support your grandstanding?"

M'Giia appeared beside me—actually between Malan and me, and she looked admiringly at Malan. "Leave him alone, David," she said. "He's making sense."

Malan smiled, then leered at me. "Trouble with your crew, Forester?"

"This isn't the simulator, Malan," I ground out. "You're over your head. M'Giia, don't pay attention to him."

M'Giia scoured me with hard eyes. "I'll do as I please. We've got to stand up to these attacks."

"Right." Malan rewarded her with a pat on the back. "When we have our own ships, we'll put the Klingons in their place!"

"Or we'll all end up dead," Jana instantly shot back, before the cheers could come again. She looked at M'Giia and asked, "You're hoping we go to war, aren't you?"

Frank hung an arm around M'Giia. "You'll get your revenge. That's the destiny of this command class. Right, everybody?"

Another cheer rose, galvanized by M'Giia's presence and sense of intense cause—unity with one of our own.

Yikes.

My hand looked about the size of a three-year-old's as I placed it on Frank Malan's chest and gave him a shove. With the other hand I pulled M'Giia away from him.

"I said leave my crew alone."

The joy of all this attention left Malan's face. He unhooked his science officer from under that six-foot arm and squared off with me, hovering over M'Giia like a vulture. "Captain Kirk's favorite little boy. You wouldn't know how to be a captain like him if a real command got dropped in your lap. We need captains like Kirk to avenge Bicea and show the Klingons we can fight back. You might as well join the Klingons, Forester. Then you can be in charge of the retreat."

"Frank," his science officer protested, and pulled

him back. "It's all right," Malan said. "I wouldn't waste my time."

M'Giia moved between us, clearly leaning toward Malan as his crew pulled him away.

"If you're the captain of the future," she said, "I'll get there by myself."

Chapter 7

Two not-particularly-good days later, I was back in Rotherot's office, and Rotherot wasn't even there.

Captain Sulu was plenty there, though.

"What's going on, Forester? Cadet M'Giia's simulator scores have dropped now. One day it's Corin, then it's Brady, and now it's M'Giia. You running a tag-team program?"

"No, sir. Her whole family died on Bicea, as you know, and she refused to take a leave of absence. Am I authorized to order her to do that, sir?"

"No, you're not." He was enjoying this, I could just tell that he was. "Your team started out with a favorable boost from Captain Kirk, but believe me, that can be lost. You're finding out about the hardest part of command—outside influences affecting your crew. You'll have to handle it. If this happened to her out in space, on a starship, you'd still have to deal with it and get her to do her job. It's as much a test for you as it is for her. That's the way the Academy sees this."

"That's . . . asking a lot of me, sir."

Oh, why did I say that?

"Her emotional condition is out of my hands, sir," I tried again, but that one wasn't much better.

Sulu nodded, at first seeming to agree with me, but somehow I didn't believe that.

"Maybe neither of you are in the right school," he said after a pause. He wasn't speaking harshly, but his words were scrubbing my skin off.

"Sir," I began hesitantly, "has the Academy been paying attention to the activities of a campus group called the Vanguard?"

"Not particularly. Why?"

"I was just wondering if those speeches constitute insubordination."

"We do discourage political involvement for cadets, but as long as they do their duty, their politics are their own affair."

"Isn't it a threat to discipline?" I asked.

"Discipline always suffers when a crewman doesn't believe in what he's doing. You can't let others affect your crew. You have to be the compass of your own crew. Know what your own beliefs are, and they'll take their strength from you."

Me, again.

"Commander Chekov's expecting you and Mr. Sturek in the bridge simulator," Captain Sulu went on, and evidently that other subject was done with. "There's a new program we want to test run before we incorporate it into the general schedule. Captain Kirk's idea."

"Yes, sir," I said, trying to refocus. "I assisted Commander Chekov this morning, installing the program. I've arranged to meet Sturek there, sir."

"And I'll be there too. Dismissed."

How could he say something so politely and easily and still have it come out like a threat? Just what seminar taught that little trick?

"Aye, sir."

In the corridor again, just as mystified as the last time. There was a pattern here.

Gear up for the simulator, this time with just Sturek and me, just a test run to make sure the graphics were on line and a shot would go where it was aimed.

Right now, that was all I wanted to do. Sit down and start shooting. Get it all out. Kill a couple of CGIs. Maybe if I got the formulations just right, Frank Malan's face would be etched on a hull plate. What a target.

The walk across Academy grounds to the simulator dome was head-clearing, but provided no answers for me. Was this what command would be like? My crew watches each other die, then has to shake off the grief and keep working? In space was there no time for mourning?

I hurried to the main starship bridge simulator and rushed into the entrance quickly enough to surprise the door panels and get a bump on the elbow for it.

Sturek crouched at the main long-range sensor

trunk on the upper deck, but there was no one else in sight.

"Good—I thought I was late!"

"You are." Commander Chekov appeared from under the helm.

I hadn't seen him!

"Where've you been?" he asked.

"Commander—I'm sorry, sir. No excuses, sir."

"I've loaded up the program and you boys will try it out as soon as Captain Sulu gets here."

Recalibrating my brain at warp speed, I nodded and met Sturek's gaze. "Aye, sir. We're ready."

"Good." Chekov stood up. "Take positions at—"

The "lift" doors opened again and Captain Sulu entered in the middle of a conversation . . . with James T. Kirk.

My feet froze. I couldn't move my feet. What was wrong with my boots?

"Because I'm shipping out on the thirtieth of this month," James Kirk was saying.

"It's just one deep-nebula navigation class," Sulu protested. "It was your idea in the first place. At least launch the seminar—"

They came onto the bridge and paused on the upper deck.

"Two weeks and that's it," Kirk said. "Get ready to sign some releases."

"Releases?"

"Well, you don't want to be held responsible, do you?"

Leaving Captain Sulu with that thought, Kirk

scanned the bridge and a touch of nostalgia warmed his ruddy cheeks.

Then he looked at Chekov. "Gentlemen? Is it loaded up?"

"Ready now, sir," the commander said. "Would you like to see the cadets attempt the action?"

Kirk almost said yes, then glanced around and seemed to be assessing the presence of his two former bridge officers and Sturek and me. What was he thinking about?

He stepped down to the command deck, circled the captain's chair, touched it, ran his hands along the back and down the arm. A chill skittered across my shoulder as if I were that chair, feeling the warmth of his reminiscence and the challenge of his presence. Sulu and Chekov both grinned sentimentally, and Sturek looked at me for just an instant. We were witnessing a precious, fleeting moment.

James Kirk gazed at the captain's chair. "Why should the cadets have all the fun?" he asked. Then he looked at Sulu and Chekov in turn. "I always wanted to have a second crack at this. What do you say, gentlemen?"

A grin broke across Sulu's face that lit up the whole bridge. The place actually got bright.

Chekov nodded firmly at his former commander and caught the enthusiasm. "Why not! It's all yours, sir!"

"All hands," Kirk said, his voice suddenly ringing, "take your posts."

What?

I figured I'd better move. So I took the helm. It was closest.

Sturek dropped from the upper starboard deck and landed in the navigation chair. That was where we'd have to sit if we were going to run the program.

A form appeared at my side and another in my periphery beside Sturek. We both looked up, and at our sides stood Sulu and Chekov. Sulu was looking down at me. Chekov was looking at Sturek.

Well, "looking" didn't exactly describe it.

"What's wrong?" Captain Kirk asked impatiently.

Chekov fanned his arms at me and Sturek. "They're in our seats!"

Kirk settled into the command chair. "Then you can be Scotty. Sulu, you be Spock. I can do this without the two of you, but I need Scotty and Spock."

"Indeed!" Captain Sulu puffed up like I didn't think he could, raised his chin and struck a pose long enough to get that word out.

"Aye-aye, Captain, sarrr!" Chekov rolled some kind of accent over the accent he already had—this was crazy.

We knew who they were talking about, of course, but *why* were they? Spock, the famous Vulcan first officer who had set a pattern for his entire race by entering Starfleet and gaining acclaim at James Kirk's side, and Captain of Engineering Montgomery Scott, whose innovations at deep-space warp engineering had provided me with something to use to smack Robin around—the legendary crew of senior officers were lesson number one for any Starfleet cadet.

Here I was, sitting in the helm chair, and behind me

was Captain James T. Kirk, the prototype of Starfleet tenacity, a man who'd been known to work every advantage until it cracked, and he wanted to play a simulator game!

Sturek surveyed me briefly from the nav seat—he didn't know what was going on either.

I flinched when the bridge around us surged to life and began to hum and click with electrical activity. Chekov must've turned it on from up there. He was standing now at the engineering station, and Sulu had climbed up to the science console and was standing there with his arms folded and one eyebrow up.

Didn't make any sense.

I glanced around at Captain Kirk just to see if these antics were some kind of a joke, and he pointed at me. "You be Sulu," he ordered, then pointed at Sturek. "And you be Chekov. I know it's asking a lot, but Academy cadets are supposed to be able to endure anything."

He settled deep into the command chair, relishing the feeling.

"Mr. Spock," he began, his voice ringing, "implement program MONAD 1701!"

"Implementing, captain," Sulu responded with an unrecognizable lilt. He worked the science board, and on several subsystems monitors and the main screen scenes popped up that I didn't recognize—old-style views of space and ship motion, and there were sounds I'd never heard before, somehow more musical than usual bridge noises.

A jolt of nostalgia hit me. All this seemed familiar . . . and it *felt* right.

"Navigator," Kirk said, "make your course six five zero mark two."

Sturek glanced at me again. He was confused too, and worried.

"Six five zero mark two, laid in, captain," he said.

"Warp factor five, helm."

My turn—

"Warp five, sir!"

"Steady as she goes."

A shiver ran my spine and a grin cracked across my face. I was really doing this! Captain James Kirk was right here! *The* Captain James Kirk was giving me orders! I'd gotten a steady-as-she-goes from James T. Kirk!

When my board changed in front of me, I almost forgot to relay the change.

"Captain, shields just snapped on! Something coming in at multiwarp speeds!"

"Yellow alert," the captain said, boiling everything down to a single action.

"Yellow alert," I responded, quite properly if I did say so myself, and the bridge panels changed to flashing amber.

"Evasive maneuvers, Mr. Sulu," Kirk added.

I parted my lips and said, "Evasive maneuvers."

Had my voice changed? I looked at the upper deck—Captain Sulu had said the same thing at the same time.

Everybody paused, looked at everybody else, and Sulu shrugged. "Habit," he threw in.

Kirk bobbed his brows once, and shrugged back.

"Extremely powerful bolt of energy coming in, captain," Sulu said then, speaking rather evenly and fluidly, but with a sense of spirit. Was that how the famous Mr. Spock sounded?

"Mr. Scott!" Kirk spoke up. "I need full shields!"

"Captain," Chekov gulped from the upper engineering station, "uh dunt ken eef we heff de powerrr!"

I gaped at Sturek. What was that supposed to be?

Kirk cranked around in his chair. "He wouldn't say that! We haven't even been hit yet!"

"Oh . . . right!" Chekov looked at his board and seemed to be enjoying himself. "I'll give it all I got, sarrr!"

On the main screen, a white globular bolt rushed toward the "ship," getting bigger and brighter, like a gigantic water balloon rolling toward us.

"It's gonna hit!" I called out, hoping I was speaking up at the right moment.

The bolt overtook the whole viewscreen, and *Slam!* The simulator bridge heaved up under us and shook to one side! At engineering, Chekov kicked over the nearest chair. Sulu jumped down from the science deck and spun the captain's chair halfway around, spinning Kirk right out of it. Kirk stuck his foot out sideways and knocked *my* chair out from under me!

All I saw as I went down was Sturek's completely baffled face and the delight of Sulu's mischievous expression. Why were they beating us up?

"Begorra!" Chekov crowed from somewhere inside a plume of exhaust from a "blown" console.

"That's Irish," Kirk scolded.

Chekov smiled and kept up that weird accent-on-accent. "Shields down to forrrty parrrcent, sarrr!"

Defensively Kirk glowered at the main screen. "Not on the first hit, they weren't," he said derisively. "Not *that* ship."

Captain Sulu climbed back to the upper deck and secured his posture in Spock-form. "We should be dead within moments. Undoubtedly this is Ensign Chekov's fault."

The "ship" shook under us again as I tried to get back into my toppled seat.

"Helm, I said evasive maneuvers!" Kirk snapped.

"We're losing power, sir!" I told him.

"Another bolt approaching, captain," Chekov said with great agitation. "Mr. Sulu is steering us right into them!"

The new hit slammed the bridge with shockwaves.

Unimpressed, Kirk simply said, "Arm torpedoes one and two."

Then he paused and looked around fitfully, troubled.

"Something's missing," he murmured.

I was looking at him, but had no idea what he could possibly be talking about. Sulu looked too, but didn't seem to have the answer either, which made me feel a little less clumsy.

"Oh, yes!" Kirk suddenly leaned to one side as if addressing himself and struck an attitude I didn't recognize. "But, Jim, you can't just open fire on an unknown spacecraft!" he rasped, then shifted to the other side of the chair. "Mind your own business,

Bones, I'm a captain, not a social worker. Mr. Chekov! Fire torpedoes!"

Sturek was completely paralyzed. The antics of the senior officers were utterly mystifying to him, and even as I was beginning to get into it, he was losing ground.

I cuffed him in the elbow, which shook him enough so that he remembered he was Chekov. He pawed his console and breathlessly responded, "Torpedoes away, sir!"

Whoosh—Whoosh—

A deadly sound, even in the simulator. Full-power photon torpedoes jetting into space, perfect killing machines with the bottled power of a solar flare. Made me wince. Imagine if those were real!

Piloting the starship in the presence of all the incarnations of the famous first crew, I indulged in a shiver of thrill and played my console as if I could sound a fanfare with it.

"Another bolt coming in, Captain," Sulu droned. "Quite illogical. I may throw up."

"Logic, my eye, Mr. Spock," Kirk tossed over. "Mr. Chekov, give me retreat coordinates."

Sturek glanced at him, then worked his board.

I turned halfway around. "Retreat, sir? That's not in the program."

His amber eyes hit me and skewered in. "Did I ask you?"

"No, sir!"

"Retreat heading laid in, sir," Sturek said.

"Helm, retreat, warp factor six."

Again I looked around. "Sir, those bolts are coming in at warp fifteen! We can't outrun them!"

He actually crossed his legs and tilted his head at me. "Are you questioning your captain's orders, cadet?"

As if I'd been punched, I gulped, "No, sir! Warp factor six! Retreat heading!"

"Navigator, effect emergency warp core dump on my mark! Three . . . two . . . one, mark!"

Taken by surprise, Sturek fumbled briefly, then found the tie-ins.

The whole bridge bumped hard, almost throwing me from my chair again.

Ffffffooooom—all screens showed a big greenish blast of contamination and every kind of crud imaginable. The computers rushed to calculate the impact, then jolted us with a second flush of shock effect.

Victory fanfare played over the sound system—the music of a technical win! He'd beaten the simulator!

Sulu came forward on the upper deck, and Chekov appeared in my periphery on the port side.

"It's dead, Jim!" they both cried out.

At the same time, with the same inflection . . . how did they know to do that?

James Kirk sank back in the command chair and moaned, "Pathetic."

Sturek was looking at his controls as if they'd grown pointed ears. "The antimatter dump caused an energy flushback . . . marvelous!"

I abandoned my board and swung around to Kirk. "You did it, sir!"

He gave a little shrug. "I had thirty years to figure it out."

"I would never think to retreat!"

"Better learn." He dismissed me as easily as that and glanced warmly around the bridge. "Thank you, gentlemen. We'll have to meet like this again sometime."

As Sulu and Chekov beamed at him happily, James Kirk rose from the command chair, then caressed the arm of the chair as if shaking hands with an old friend. For a moment, neither Sturek nor I dared disturb his reverie. He'd just given us a gift, and to rupture his moment of peace would've been improper.

As I watched one of the most famous men in Federation history move about only steps from me, I sensed a loneliness no one had ever mentioned. Were captains lonely?

He pulled himself away from the chair in one of the saddest moments of strength I'd ever witness, and headed for the upper deck lift doors, and didn't look back.

I paused, waiting for him to cast one last glance, but he didn't.

In those four or five seconds, I learned a hard lesson.

"Captain—"

Pushing out of my chair, I hurried to the upper deck so he wouldn't have to look down again.

He turned. "Question?"

"What's it like," I began, "when the ships out there are really trying to kill you?"

James Kirk, the unexploitable, glanced at Captain Sulu, then at Commander Chekov, down at Sturek through a cloud of fritzing smoke, and finally back at me. Harnessed anticipation crossed between the two of us.

"You'll find out," he said.

Chapter 8

"Corin, you'll have to figure out some way to short-cut those firing sequences and coordinate them with Jana's course plottings. Robin, I don't see any way around your giving us more accurate numbers on the warp core surges. You'll have to shave it down one more decimal point on each of these scales. Sturek, maybe you can help him by trimming the sensor shifts, and I'll concentrate on applying a few of the more advanced strategical maneuvers and making my orders more specific to each degree. M'Giia, if you could . . . M'Giia?"

"Yes?"

"Are you listening?"

"Of course. Why wouldn't I be?"

Sounded all right when she said it fast, but she'd been looking at that viewscreen, and Frank Malan and his crew were over there.

I'd decided to go over our latest simulation exercises in the cadet lounge, because—well, I didn't have a very good reason. Except they seemed to act more at ease in here than anywhere else, and I needed them to be at ease with each other for at least ten minutes a day. At least they'd be paying attention to me, or so I'd thought.

And it was cool in here, something we needed after a very hot day. We'd spent all morning in the simulator, then noon cleaning up what we'd done all morning, then all afternoon on the cross-country obstacle course, carrying water-soaked logs over our heads. That was the Academy's way of expanding our minds while destroying our bodies.

Then, of course, we had to write up reports of how it felt and analyze our own mistakes. And for free time, which was now, we got to analyze our miserable destruction of the simulator. A well-rounded day, all in all.

The Starfleet News Service was playing on the big screen again, running through the day's business as it pertained to Starfleet, and every other story had something to do with the activity—all right, slaughter—on Bicea Colony.

Scheduling at the Academy was very tight. We had full weekdays from reveille at zero-six hundred to evening drills, and only after showers and study hours could we break to the lounge, so that's what almost everybody did at least twice a week. The lounge building not only housed the lounge, but the Olympic pool, the indoor track, and an arcade of hand-eye coordination games. Even when we weren't training, we still were.

And, of course, the lounge was where we could just sit and stare at a great big screen and if we didn't want to look at the screen we could look at Frank Malan.

Another command decision I could polish and hang on my barrack wall.

My nerves were still buzzing from those hot-wired minutes at James Kirk's helm, making it torture to level out and concentrate on keeping my crew banded together. After every surge of thrill came a shudder borne up by those last three words he'd left me with. *You'll find out.*

Somehow he'd managed to inspire me and terrify me in the same breath.

"Listen to this!"

I didn't recognize the voice, but I knew that tone, and instantly looked up at the wide screen. A huge flock of cadets was watching now, and Frank Malan and his troglodyte troopers were right up front.

On the screen, Commandant Rotherot was making another announcement.

"—and the president of the Federation has issued a formal apology to the Klingons over Starfleet's aggressive actions as incurred by the *U.S.S. Sentinel*. The Klingon High Council accepted that the exchange of weapons fire was based upon a misunderstanding—"

"Misunderstanding!" Frank Malan roared. "The Federation sold out Starfleet! They apologized to those butchers!"

"That's pretty extreme, Malan," I said, loudly enough for most of the cadets to hear.

Okay, I'd probably end up with my spinal column holding up one end of the volleyball net, but they ought to hear a dissenting opinion from someplace, right? At least hear it.

"Face it," I added. "You're jumping to conclusions. The Federation isn't ready to blame the Klingons for Bicea."

"Easy talk from somebody who won't get involved," M'Giia coldly accused.

Malan moved through the crowd and stood beside M'Giia's chair. "You ought to stick up for your own crewmate, at least, Forester. The Federation's a pack of wimps, allowing the Klingons to massacre our families."

"That theory doesn't hold water," I told him. "Klingon colonies on the Neutral Zone are being attacked too."

He pointed at me. "Those are just rumors started by the Klingons to cover their tracks."

He started to say something else, but Captain Sulu's voice came over the comm. "Cadet Malan, report with your crew to the planetarium."

Opening the communicator, he said, "Malan here. Aye, sir," and waved for his crew to gather. In the few seconds it took to assemble them, he patted M'Giia on the shoulder. "We're behind you, even if your own crew isn't."

"Thank you, Frank," she said.

"M'Giia!" I attempted. "Our futures are on the line. We've got our own work to worry about, and I want you to ignore what he's saying."

"Ignoring things got my family killed." Her voice was as flat as the floor, cooler than Sturek could even manage. "I know how to survive."

"Yeah, she knows," Malan agreed. He took her arm and led her out of the lounge, flocked by his training crew and a couple of other crews. "Forester, keep your losers away from us."

The lounge fell into a tense peace, and on the big screen was a report about the Academy marching musical corps.

There went Malan, and M'Giia was with him.

"That lady is going to blow like a volcano one of these days," Corin said, following them out with his gaze.

"I'm worried about her," Jana admitted.

Robin glanced furtively at each of us. "Maybe she's just taking it really well. She's so under control . . . "

"That's not under control," I told him. "That's over-control, and I don't think it'll hold."

Corin leaned forward with his elbows on his knees. "I got my scores up and Robin got his up, and now we got this. You'd better come up with something to break her out of it," he suggested, "or all our hard work is going right out the airlock."

"We can't let her fall apart," Jana said.

Beside her, Sturek nodded, but said nothing.

"She won't fall apart," I assured, as if I knew.

Jana shot me a warning glare. "Andorians are prickly, David. This ice-queen act is bizarre."

"She's a diplomat's daughter," I tried. "Maybe she's just bearing up."

"She's paying a price," Corin said. "We're all gonna pay it if we don't get her to break out."

Now my communicator chirped and Commander

Chekov's voice made a terse order. "Cadet Forester, report to the science lab Delta Tango."

I flipped open the communicator. "Forester, acknowledged."

Corin was still looking at me. They all were.

Spreading my hands, I complained, "Come on! I'm a team commander, not a priest!"

"She just needs an excuse to blow off steam," Jana said. "You could think of something, couldn't you?"

Corin cuffed me in the knee. "Where's that command thinking, huh?"

Sturek buffeted the moment with a loaded expression of sympathy and doubt. Jana kept glaring at me. Robin's eyes were wide with anticipation.

Yeah. Where was it?

Lab Delta Tango was in the Cornwell Systems Analysis Building, and getting there across the breadth of the Academy grounds sucked up a good ten minutes, all of which were clogged with everything from therapy to a good slap for M'Giia. What did I know about the psychological repercussions of bottled grief? I'd never even had a pet cat die. My cat was eighteen and still mousing.

I hurried down the stark white corridor of the Sys-An building and went all the way to Lab Delta Zebra before I realized I'd gone too far. Doubling back, I broke into a run and surged through the doors of Delta Tango at full skid.

And inside—well, of course—was Captain Kirk. Why not?

Commander Chekov was there too. They both looked up in time to see me bump into a sink. Nice going, Grace.

"Good morning, Captain!" I blurted to cover my stumble. "Morning, Commander—"

"Morning," Kirk responded. "You in the mood for a privilege, Forester?"

"Oh . . . at your service, sir."

"Come over here."

If only I could get there without skinning a knee—

He held out a computer cartridge. "I've got something that's got to stay in this room. This isn't Academy business. This is Starfleet business. Top security classification. Understood?"

I looked at Chekov, but he wasn't offering any clues. His eyes were gleaming, though, as if he was proud of me. A voice in the back of my head kept murmuring *garbage scow, garbage scow.*

"Top security, sir?" I asked. "You mean, command cadets only?"

"I mean Starfleet senior flight officers only," Captain Kirk corrected, and that was a heck of a correction. He'd leaped about as far from cadets as he could get without bringing in the Admiralty. "This is for real captains to practice on, cadet."

Real captains, practicing. The whole idea hit me with unexpected impact. I'd always imagined that the learning process ended with command of a ship— guess not.

Kirk was standing there, waiting. So was Chekov. Next move seemed to be mine.

"Understood very clearly, sir," I told him with what I hoped was a decisive tone.

"You've been assisting Mr. Chekov with the installation of the new simulator matrices. I want you to help him with this one, and make it a priority." He handed me the computer cartridge. "These are the design and weaponry specs on a new Klingon heavy cruiser. I want you to incorporate them into a simulator program and give it a top security code status with the access code 'Sultan's Great Day.'"

The cartridge was warm in my hand. I looked at it rather foolishly. "Sultan's Great Day. Aye, sir. Captain . . . why are we war-gaming a ship that belongs to an empire we're trying to make peace with? And why use the Academy's simulator instead of the real starships?"

He eyed me with a dangerous sidelong gaze. Ouch.

"Because there are possibilities we need to prepare for that we shouldn't *look* like we're preparing for," he said. "Carry on, Mr. Forester."

He glanced at Chekov one more time, then strode with great self-satisfaction toward the door and out into the corridor.

Had M'Giia been right all along? Was Starfleet preparing us for war even as the Federation jockeyed for passivity? Was one a cover for the other?

"What's wrong with you today?" Chekov sidled toward me.

"Oh . . . few problems with my crew, sir."

"Skill?" he asked. "Technical? Station postings?"

"Personal, sir."

"Ah. There's no manual for that."

"No, sir."

"Trouble with your Vulcan?"

"Sturek? Oh, no, sir. Why do you ask?"

"Sometimes there's trouble with Vulcans," he said with a wise shrug that explained exactly nothing.

My shoulder actually went up a notch, trying to imitate that shrug. Must be some kind of officers' secret shrug.

"Your Mr. Sturek is in Lab Delta India right now," Chekov told me. "He's working on fragments from the ship that attacked Bicea."

Suddenly interested, I took a rather impolite step toward him. "I thought it was a Klingon ship!"

That shrug again. "We have the fragments . . . might as well analyze them."

"Commander, how did we get fragments of a ship that got away?"

"Captain Kirk went out yesterday and scoured the atmosphere and the ruins of the settlement. He found bits of the attack ship broken off by planetary defenses. There is no match to any metallurgy on the planet, so we're going to the next step."

"Why Sturek?" I asked. "Why use cadets at all on something this big?"

"*Because* it's big," he answered cryptically. "No one knows the research is being done here. We can have peace and quiet, and keep our eyes on you. And because Captain Kirk trusts Vulcans. He's funny that way. Now, specifically with your crewman, what's the trouble?"

For a moment I paused, not knowing whether he

was asking as a commander or as an adviser. I'd had both, but they were always different people. What was his role here at command school? Were the courtesies different?

Well, after all, he did ask, didn't he?

"My communications specialist lost her family in the Bicea attack. It's eating her inside out, but she's not letting us help. She's just going on with her training as if nothing happened. It's a lot harder to manage a crew than it looked in the manuals."

"Of course," Chekov allowed. "Starfleet gives the most challenging cadets to the most capable command school students. Bringing out the best in them will bring out the best in you. It's an old Russian technique. Captain Kirk saw something in you, and something in the way your team acted out their roles during the mock terrorist attack. I've seen him do that before, but only twice in all these years. One of those command cadets is now a Fleet starship first officer, and his entire training crew is still with him. The other team . . . they washed out. All of them together."

Was there something wrong with the temperature control in here?

"You're saying," I began, "that my crew has no options. We stay together and deal with whatever comes. Sink or swim."

"Smart boy."

I shook my head. "But I don't know what to do. I can handle the technical aspects of their work, but how do I break through shells like the one M'Giia's putting up around herself?"

Chekov leaned on the sink counter and held up an illustrative finger. "Before I joined the crew of the *Enterprise*, I served aboard a survey ship with a commanding officer like that. Very hot temper, but she thought getting angry was unprofessional. As long as she exploded from time to time, she was the most charming person on board. If she held back . . . uch! If you want to help your communications officer, get her to express herself *outside* the simulator."

"I can't pick a fight with her, sir! It's against regulations—it's against . . . just . . . and the crew's personality problems aren't really the commander's domain, are they?"

"Everything that happens on the ship is the commander's domain. A captain who pays attention to the temperament and morale of his crew can count on that crew when he really needs them. 'A captain who pushes his crew out of the nest will have a crew who really flies.' Another old Russian saying."

Casting him a pathetic, mournful sort of look, I muttered, "Old Russians never had to deal with Andorians."

He shrugged. "Suit yourself. If you've made it to command school, you've probably made someone mad before. So . . . do it again."

"Thank you, sir . . . "

"Thank me after your scores go up. Let's get this heavy cruiser onto the simulator. We're going to need it."

Pushing off the counter, he tapped the cartridge I was holding.

The cartridge lay in my hand passively, stirring

curious questions and reaching out much farther than this lab.

A Klingon warship, different from those before it, a new heavy cruiser that the Klingons shouldn't even be building, given the stipulations of the treaty with the Federation. Code name: Sultan's Great Day.

I held it up. "Sir, does this mean the Klingons are Starfleet's next target?"

Chekov strode toward the computer complex in the middle of the lab and without looking back at me waved a hand.

"Never mind what it means."

Installing the new Klingon heavy cruiser program took the entire rest of the day and half the night with just the commander and me working on it. We couldn't ask for help, because the whole thing was classified.

The rest of the night I barely slept, tortured by night thoughts of Klingons and failure, M'Giia and war, command and washing out. When reveille sounded, I was relieved to roll out and put an end to the long jumbled hours.

Drill, breakfast, then simulator. And no sign of Sturek.

He was always present at drill and breakfast, but not today. Was he still in the lab, working on those ship fragments? Maybe that was why Captain Kirk liked Vulcans—stamina.

I dragged myself to the main bridge simulator, and my team was already there, which I was glad to note. As a commander, I'd rather have been last to arrive than first and have to scoop up my crew from six different places.

Corin was at his helm, playing with the new programming. Jana was on her knees at the base of her navigation console, closing the access panel. Over at engineering, Robin played his board like a piano, though I had no idea what he was doing since we hadn't started yet. At least he seemed more contented than the last time I'd seen him. M'Giia hovered over the science station, which would've been Sturek's place if he'd been here. That was her job—take over science if the science officer went down or fainted or got a cramp or something.

"Okay, crew," I greeted them, pushing off my fatigue, "Ready to take on the Klingons?"

M'Giia turned. "I wish it wasn't just a simulation. I'd like to pulverize them for real."

Rather than dropping to the command deck, I moved along the upper deck toward her. "I don't like that attitude, M'Giia. This isn't doing you any good."

"What isn't?" Her brows came down.

"As long as you act this way, you're putting us all at risk, and I want you to stop. Get help or do whatever it takes. Going into missions with suppressed rage endangers us all."

"This is fake!" She swept her hand along the science console. "It's a simulator!"

"Someday it'll be real," I provoked. "And you'll kill us all."

A purple vein hardened on her neck. "Are you trying to start a fight?"

"You're an Andorian. You haven't got the guts for a fight."

"I've done nothing to endanger our standings!"

The space between us closed. "I think you have."

"Start the simulator and I'll show you there's no cause to worry!"

"We'll start when I'm satisfied we can *all* work at peak efficiency and not a moment before."

"You want efficiency?" Her eyes flared and her antennae went stiff and straight.

She reared back and let fly a purposeful punch, awkward but plenty effective as her sharp fist drove into my stomach.

"Aw—" I choked and doubled over. I'd braced for a slap in the jaw!

The punch drove the air from my lungs and I slid to one knee.

"M'Giia!" Jana dropped what she was doing and vaulted to the upper deck, where she held M'Giia back.

Corin knelt beside me. "Wow—David, you okay?"

"Jana!" M'Giia gulped. "Let go of me!"

As he kept me from toppling over, Corin looked up at her. "Why don't you leave him alone? You're losing control!"

"It's okay, Geoff," I gasped. "Wasn't really . . . M'Giia doing the . . . hitting . . ."

M'Giia pulled out of Jana's grasp and knelt in front of me.

"David . . . I'm sorry. I didn't mean to hit you!"

As I blinked at her through watery eyes, I saw the

sheath of coldness peel off, revealing a pain in her eyes and a regret in her manner.

"I've been bottling up," she said. "I never thought I'd take it out on anyone."

"Feel better now?" I asked.

She shook her head and sighed. "I don't know . . . I don't know."

She and Corin helped me to my feet, and Corin said, "Can I hit you now? Maybe we can bring up my scores too."

Chapter 9

Navigation class. One of the most critical elements of the education process at the Academy, and I was having trouble paying attention. Hadn't seen Sturek in a couple days and I was starting to get concerned. Was he sacrificing his training and his attendance to Academy work in order to analyze a scrap of metal from some ship, just to find out it was the Klingons, as we suspected all along?

How could the senior officers demand that he give up so much of his precious training time? Why didn't they just get Starfleet scientists to do their work? Why drain Sturek and my whole team in the process?

Why didn't I ask?

Captain Kirk was right here, right now, hovering over a large table cluttered with old-style laminated ocean navigation charts, and most of the command candidate team leaders were clustered around him as he demonstrated how to read the two-dimensional charts.

So why didn't I just open my big mouth and ask?

"Starfleet Command kicked like mules when I made them put ocean navigation in the Academy curriculum," Captain Kirk was saying. "Wait till I tell 'em I want naked-eye signal recognition." He plucked through the charts, picking up several and putting them back down. "Where's Chesapeake Bay?"

Beside him, Commander Chekov didn't miss a beat. "Between Baltimore and Norfolk, sir."

Grinning, Chekov held up a rolled chart.

Kirk needled him with a glare, then snatched the chart.

"All due respect, sir," Frank Malan began from the other side of the table—he and I were as far apart as we could get and still be in the same class. "We'll never be out on an ocean."

Chekov looked up. "You'll be on one next semester, cadet."

"But why?"

Kirk tapped the laid-out charts with the rolled one. "Before you learn to navigate in three dimensions, you should know how to navigate in two."

"But what good would that do in space?" Malan persisted.

To my dismay, I found myself agreeing and said, "We've got positional verification guidance on starships, sir."

James Kirk tortured me with a long death-ray glare. "Do we?"

Oh, God . . .

"Sorry, captain," I muttered.

"And who says you'll command a starship?" he went on, still drilling me.

I glanced around at the other command candidates. "Well . . . every commander wants a starship, sir . . . ."

"What would you want a starship for?"

Hoping to make up, I straightened and said, "They're the most important ships around, sir!"

"If you think that way, Forester," he drawled, "I hope you never command one."

"Odds are with you there," Malan shoved in, enjoying my predicament.

I shot him a glare behind the captain's back, but Kirk didn't miss it. He was still looking at me.

"It's not the ship. It's the captain and crew," he said. "There are twelve ships of the line in Starfleet, dozens of support ships, and thousands of specific-duty craft. In the private sector, there are millions more. Freighters, tankers, tugs, merchants, frigates—and they're all important. If the captain of a lightship makes a mistake, the crew of a starship might pay with their lives. If a starship's grounded, a whole sector could be crippled. Right down to a barge crewman on sensor watch, everybody's important in space." He released me from the glare, and looked at Chekov, grumbling, "We should have a field trip about that. Seems to be the hardest thing to learn."

Chekov grinned. "I'll tell Command you're volunteering to teach it, sir."

"You'll be carrying my gear."

"Captain," Frank Malan interrupted, "there's something going on with the Klingons, isn't there? More than we're being told by Starfleet News. The Klingons have never fully abided by the Organian Peace Treaty. Why don't we put an end to them once and for all?"

"Nice and simple," Kirk agreed. "Well, if you're looking for simple solutions, cadet, you're in the wrong place. And I think we'd take it personally if the Klingons thought the same way about us."

Malan held out a hand and balled it into a fist. "What's it really *like* out there?"

Kirk surveyed him wisely. "It isn't *like* anything, cadet." He put the Chesapeake Bay chart down on the others and pointed up, out, toward the ceiling, the sky. Space.

"Out there," he said, "out there, whether we like it or not, we have enemies. And you're the ones who will have to deal with them. I've heard some cadets say the Klingons are unthinking animals. Well, I'm here to tell you it's not true. Animals don't run star empires. The Klingons may appear brutal, but they also have a deeply rooted code of honor. Study it. Understand it. Know your enemy."

Enemy. He'd come right out and said it. Did he mean what we thought he meant? What we saw boiling in Frank Malan's delighted face right now?

"Sir," I began, "can I ask . . . "

Kirk turned toward me, and when I paused he prodded, "Ask what?"

"Do you . . . believe in always following regulations to the letter, or in violating them when the situation needs it?"

From across the table Malan stared at me, apparently not believing that I'd actually dared to ask that question. Couldn't believe it myself, really. But I had to know.

Would a man like James Kirk even tell me? He'd gotten his knowledge the hard way, paid with his own blood and the blood of his crewmen. Would he share it just because I asked?

Suddenly I felt like a coward to want the shortcut.

Kirk eyed Chekov and they shared a silent communication. They knew Kirk's methods, and so did every cadet here. Without meaning to, I'd put Kirk on the hot seat.

After a pointed moment, Kirk looked at me. "Are there some regulations you're planning on violating, cadet?"

Oh, now what?

"Uh . . . no, sir! Not at all, sir."

He held me in that mischievous glare of his and said, "Too bad."

Oh, now, what did *that* mean!

Letting me off the hook with a hint of a smile, Kirk said, "Regulations are for perfect situations. It's up to you to make them fit imperfect ones. That's why we don't send computers out into space to make decisions. We go with them. We temper them with instinct and improvisation. That's what we do best. The Academy can teach you how to apply the regulations to regular moments, but life in space is made up of thousands of hours of boredom offset by moments of abject terror. When that time hits, it'll be you, and not regulations, dealing with it."

A brief silence chased his words, and once the realization sank in that he was done talking, the cadets spontaneously erupted into applause.

Standing there like a mannequin, I couldn't clap. I was exhausted from those words. I just stared and stared. He'd given us a whole career in one paragraph!

"Forester," Kirk said, and I held my breath, "take these charts down to lab Delta India and have Mr. Sturek help you feed them into the holodeck simulators in the Sanford Building. Tomorrow we'll have a navigational seminar that none of you will ever forget. Next semester," he added, pointing out the tall windows at the open waters of San Francisco Bay, "you get the real thing. Cadets, dismissed."

"David! David!"

Halfway to the lab, I stopped at the call of Robin Brady's voice, and turned to see him running toward me up the long, breezy sidewalk that led down to the athletic grounds.

"Robin! Calm down! What's wrong?"

He skidded to a stop. "I went to one of the Vanguard meetings!"

"What?" I almost dropped the laminated charts, and he caught them and stuffed them back into my arms. "Why would you do that?"

"I thought . . . it was Faith's idea. She said maybe I should get involved with a group on campus."

"Robin, not *them*!" I wailed.

"I know, I know, just another bonehead mistake. I

won't go back. But, David," he said, grasping my arm, "I saw M'Giia there."

Trouble on trouble. I stepped back to get a good square look at him. "Are you sure? It wasn't another Andorian?"

"She didn't see me, but it was her. And she fit in real well with those guys. She was hanging around with Frank Malan and a couple of his command crew. She was the only non-human there, but they still accepted her. Why would they accept an Andorian?"

"With their attitude, I don't know. So the real question is, what do they want from her?"

He shrugged. "She was telling them how she thought the Klingons should pay for the massacres along the Neutral Zone."

I shook my head. "And having an Andorian daughter of an ambassador on their side could give them credibility."

"Yeah."

"Okay, Robin, I'll keep my eyes open. But from now on, stay away from the Vanguard, okay?"

"I will! I will . . . they wouldn't let me back in anyway."

"How do you know?"

"Well . . . I didn't last very long before they figured me out. They've got a telepath to determine who's a true Vanguard supporter. Once she looked into my mind, they started being careful what they said around me."

"All right. I'll handle it. Just don't go back there."

"I won't."

* * *

A new twist, and it was pinching. M'Giia and the Vanguard. And Robin going to a meeting like that just because Faith Gage told him to. I was losing my grip on my crew before I even got a grip on them.

My mind was in six places as I hurried across the campus to the labs. The Academy research and class facilities were laid out according to old-style ocean signal flags. Building Delta was a science lab facility. Each of its labs was a different signal flag. Delta Alfa, Delta Bravo and so on. Same with the other buildings—the phys ed facility had gym Bravo Alfa, Bravo Charlie, and on like that. The planetarium's annex classrooms and holodecks were Papa Alfa, and on down. The Sanford Flight Simulation Complex was shorted to Sierra Alfa, Sierra Bravo, Sierra Charlie. The only signal flag missing would be the redundant one—there was no gym Bravo Bravo or flight sim deck Lima Lima.

Generally the system worked very well and gave us all a sense of organization and security. It also taught us all the signal codes, which were also used in subspace flight communications training. The simple alphabetical code was still Earth's primary method of flight identification, and the consistency had served long and well, allowing pilots both young and old to understand each other.

It gave me a little anchor to cling to in this whirlwind of problems with Robin and M'Giia and everything else facing us down right now. I was very uneasy with Faith Gage's influence on Robin—imagine making someone that shy, that reclusive, go to a meeting of people like Frank Malan. What kind of power did she have over him?

Lab Delta India was one of the smaller labs, and that was probably the reason Captain Kirk had arranged for Sturek to use it. Privacy. In spite of the security of Sturek's project, the door opened right up as I walked toward it. No lock. Was that for the sake of appearance?

I hoped so as I strode in, wrestling two dozen rolled laminated ocean nav charts.

And there wasn't anybody in here.

"Sturek? Are you here?"

From a room around a partition and through a doorway, he called, "Yes, David, in chemical electro-spectral analysis. One moment, please."

I didn't go in there. Electro-spectral analysis could be touchy. Even the movement of a person walking past could disrupt—

A loud noise blew my thoughts right out of my head and the laminated charts out of my arms. The charts flew upward, rattling in the air, and scattered to the floor, and I went down among them, driven back and down by a firm hand of repercussion.

Explosion!

Chapter 10

As I struggled to my feet, skidding on the laminated charts, a gout of toxic green smoke boiled from the electrospectral analysis chamber, and a sign over the door flashed Danger! Contamination! Do Not Enter!

"Sturek!" I coughed his name and scrambled toward the electro chamber, just as behind me the main door opened and Kirk and Sulu walked in.

No time for formalities—I ignored them.

I heard Kirk's voice— "Toxic! Keep back!"

He might've been shouting at me, or at Sulu. It didn't matter—I was already inside the green cloud, holding my breath and keeping my eyes clamped shut.

"Sturek! Can you hear me?"

The desire to open my eyes was overwhelming, the need to take a breath even worse. I knew neither would do me any good and forced myself to move by feel, faltering with every step, holding my breath until my lungs screamed.

Just when my lungs turned to scrambled eggs, my hands bumped a recognizable form on the deck. I shoved my fingers into the fabric and flesh, closed them like claws, and hauled away.

Sturek was limp at first, then stirred enough to get one leg under him and together we shoved ourselves our feet.

A forced cough bolted out of my chest—I couldn't help it—and acrid chemical smoke surged back into my lungs. My head instantly swam, and I gagged. My guts turned inside out.

Dragging Sturek, I scraped back the way I'd come, hoping luck would bring me to the invisible doorway.

"This way, Forester!"

I angled toward the sound. Good thing—I'd have run headlong into a wall if he hadn't called out. A surge of heat scored my left cheek—fire!

Flames nipped at my elbow and shoulder. I pivoted Sturek away from them and tried to straighten up.

The wall skimmed the top of my head, and flames licked at my left elbow and hip as I turned and dragged Sturek, both of us choking, out into the main lab. My eyes burned and watered, and at my side Sturek grew heavier and slipped to the floor, pulling me to my knees.

"David—" he choked. "Proof—inside!"

"What proof?" I gagged back.

"The attacking ship—Bicea—" He tried to speak, and was thrown into a fit of coughing.

Thick hands grabbed me and pulled me farther from the green smoke, then all the way out into the corridor, while alert klaxons bellowed around us. I twisted hard, trying in a fit of incoherence to get back in there to pull Sturek out, but Captain Sulu appeared in my way, with Sturek firmly in tow.

Sulu put Sturek down beside me, leaning against the far corridor wall, and Captain Kirk knelt at my side while I hacked out the bad air.

Seconds later, the corridor rumbled with footsteps and a hazardous materials team thundered past us and into the lab, dressed in full-body protective suits and fire-control gear. They'd lock it down . . . .

"What happened?" Kirk demanded.

"Explosion, sir," I rasped as sparks floated past us from the lab.

Sturek grasped my arm. "Proof—"

I looked at Kirk and blinked the hot sting out of my eyes. "Sir, he found something . . . about Bicea . . . that ship . . . the proof's burning up . . . "

"Let it burn. We'll find other proof," Captain Kirk assured. "It's not worth your lives."

"Forester," Sulu said sharply, "you broke procedure by going into a toxic environment. You should've let the haz-mat team go in after Mr. Sturek. Risking two lives is unacceptable judgment, Cadet." He looked at Captain Kirk. "Tell him, Captain."

Kirk adjusted me against the wall so I could breathe, and glanced at Sulu. "You broke every rule we've got, Forester," he said. "Good job."

"It had to be a bomb," Sulu said, blinking into the smoke. "Nothing in there would explode on its own. We'll have to investigate this. And you, Mr. Sturek."

Sturek shoved himself into a better position and gaped at Sulu as if he didn't understand at first.

I sat up straight. "Are you suggesting he blew himself up, sir?"

Sulu tipped his head in doubt. "There are kamikazes in every war."

"I challenge that, sir!"

"So would I," Kirk said.

Dismayed, Sulu looked at him, then at me, and seemed to realize what he was up against. "All right. I'll confine him to quarters pending investigation."

Straightening up a little more, I gulped, "I protest, sir!"

"Noted. He'll have permission to work with the team. But no other contact."

"No contact, sir?"

Sulu skewered me with one of those looks. "I thought I was speaking English. Would you like to hear it in Klingon?"

Backing off, I uttered, "No, sir."

Sturek was dazed and now seemed shocked. He nodded, but made no more coherent response.

"Do you understand?" Sulu asked firmly.

With a troubled glance at me, his face pasty and pinched, Sturek nodded again.

"I understand . . . . "

Limping, coughing, and sore, I made my way across the twilight grounds to the cadet lounge. My crew would be there—except Sturek. Resentment boiled in my chest—I knew why Kirk and Sulu had confined Sturek to quarters pending investigation. They wanted him to keep working on identifying that Bicea ship. They wanted him to replicate whatever "proof" he'd found about its origin, and he couldn't do that in the brig, or even while attending classes. He'd have to sacrifice this whole semester if an answer wasn't found soon.

Was that what it meant to be in Starfleet? Sacrifice?

Maybe, but I didn't have to feel good about it, not when it came to one of my crew who'd been pinned to work on something he shouldn't have to work on.

They said they'd take Sturek's record into consideration. Sounded good, but that could mean anything.

Hopes for a peaceful evening among friends blew sky high when I limped into the lounge and heard what I heard.

"The latest outrage is this explosion at Starfleet Academy. This 'mysterious' laboratory explosion is the latest in a series of deceptions from Starfleet. Vital evidence about the ship that attacked Bicea is destroyed and we're supposed to believe that's a coincidence? It's time we knew the truth!"

Well, its wasn't Frank Malan talking, but it was his sentiment.

No—this person was on the main viewscreen, being interviewed.

Crowded cadets responded with murmuring whispers and disturbed comments as I sifted through them toward my crewmates.

"David," Jana instantly said, "have you been hearing this? This is the spokesman for the Vanguard. Remember about them?"

"He has a right to his opinion," M'Giia told her.

I glanced at M'Giia, but she kept watching the screen.

"The explosion destroyed evidence that we believe linked the Klingons to the savage attacks along the Neutral Zone," the Vanguard speaker continued. "Why would Starfleet send vital information all the way to Earth to be analyzed at Starfleet Academy when any starship could do the analysis? Why not a civilian scientist in a proper Federation laboratory? Because the public can believe a student might accidentally blow himself up, that's why! What better way to hide the truth!"

"Who is this guy?" I mumbled as other cadets also mumbled around me.

"But Starfleet made a critical error!" the Vanguard person said. "The one who was at the lab was a Vulcan cadet! And we all know Vulcans are barely more than living machines. They're incapable of making mistakes! It's all part of a plot by alien members of the Federation to betray us to the Klingons and depose humanity from its proper place at the head of the Federation!"

"*What?*" I gasped. "Is he kidding?"

"I can't believe they're broadcasting this," Jana seethed.

"They're saying Sturek blew up the lab on purpose!" Corin blurted.

"And the evidence about those attacks," Robin added quietly.

Jana pulled my arm. "Is Sturek all right?"

"He's fair. How are the rest of you holding up?"

The best I got was a shrug from Robin.

M'Giia shouldered away from me and went closer to the viewscreen, much too attentive to the Vanguard speaker's words.

Robin was watching her too, and glanced at me, but I shook my head. *Not here, not now.*

"I don't know what she sees in that bonehead talk," Corin grumbled. "I know she's hurting, but this is rotten."

"Even though Starfleet Academy has stonewalled our requests for information," the Vanguard guy went on, waving his arms like a preacher, "we know he was working on the Bicea incident and we demand disclosure! We demand the Vulcan cadet be dismissed from the Academy as a security risk!"

A cheer surged up from the forest of cadets to my right, and in the middle of them—it figured—Frank Malan.

I was a little gratified that most of the other cadets looked disgusted, but only a little.

"Sturek almost got killed!" Corin wailed. "And they want to hang him out to dry!"

"We've got to help him," Jana declared.

Motioning to keep our voices down, I pulled Jana away and Corin and Robin came along with us.

"We can't interfere in the investigation!" I said. "We'll only complicate things."

"Starfleet isn't above political pressures," Jana insisted. "What if they get rid of Sturek just to end the controversy? What if they start discharging cadets every time trouble pops up?"

"They won't. Captain Sulu—"

"Is only here until his ship is ready for deep space," Corin filled in. "Then it'll be Rotherot. And you know what he's like. He's a desk jockey. Politics'll scare a guy like that."

"Or someone at Starfleet Command could put pressure on Captain Sulu," Robin suggested. Man, for somebody with a quiet voice, he sure did seem loud.

Jana put both hands out conspiratorially. "We can break into the lab and find out what really happened."

"If Jana and I agree," Corin said, "it's got to be a good idea."

"If you two agree," I impugned, "it's probably a sign the world is coming to an end. We could get caught so fast—"

"If we get caught," Jana said, "it'll be a sign that cadets stick together!"

Glaring at her, I asked, "Are you so certain that Sturek is being sacrificed? Are you willing to get court martialled on that chance? We have to find *legal* ways to help Sturek."

"Oh? How?" Frustrated, Jana put her hands on her hips. "Things would be different if I were calling the shots."

"Well, you're not."

My feet were cold in my boots as I looked at each of them and saw what was in their faces—would I abandon them too when things got tough? Would I sacrifice their lives so the rules could stay unruptured?

A pretty good question. Was there a Ouija board nearby?

I lowered my voice even more. "As team commander, I have legal access to some parts of the Academy computer," I said. "If we look carefully in the morning, while computer activity is at its peak, our search will be covered. We might find something about Sturek's project."

"I can do that," Robin said eagerly.

"I'll help!" Corin tossed in.

Now my hands were cold too as I looked at Jana.

"And tonight," I said, "we'll break into the lab and see if there are any clues."

Jana jumped a foot. "Yes!"

Corin slapped me on the back. Robin grinned tentatively.

Regulations are for regular times . . . .

The Delta labs were dark and quiet, smelling slightly of smoke and chemicals. Fire retardants, probably, spilled out into the corridor. It squished on the soaked carpet as I led Corin, Robin, and Jana down the dim corridor, lit only by tiny blue courtesy lights running along the floorboards.

None of this seemed real, until I saw the yellow Security Only tape blocking off the doorway of Delta India. We really *were* breaking the law.

Somehow the Academy had always seemed separate from conventional law, because we had so many of our own rules and regulations, so regimented a life that there was little tolerance of any cracks, and those inclined to break the rules were weeded out the first year.

So what was my excuse?

"Bad idea," I mumbled as I stepped between the yellow tapes and ducked into the lab itself.

The ceiling was melted, looked more like a cave ceiling, complete with stalactites of semi-liquidized insulation. Blackened walls were barely recognizable as walls. Our eyes adjusted to the tiny courtesy lights, now working only on one side of the lab, but the room didn't resemble a lab anymore and we had a hard time finding our way through the mess. At first I didn't even recognize the entrance to the electrospectral analysis lab, but after feeling my way along the black wall, I found the entry. The doorframe was actually bent.

I thought of Sturek. How could anyone think he would do that to himself?

"Quiet!" Jana gasped suddenly. "I think I hear something!"

Robin started shaking. "Maybe we shouldn't . . . "

"Mr. Forester."

The sound of Captain Sulu's voice was a shock, but not entirely a surprise. My whole body turned cold now as the sheen of portable scene lights popped on, nearly blinding my crew.

As we squinted, we saw Captain Sulu and Commander Chekov step out of the lavatory alcove.

"I expected better from you," Sulu said. "We were hoping to catch the real criminals."

"Sir!" I stumbled toward him and slipped on the melted laminate of one of Kirk's coastal charts. "Sir, we're just trying to clear our crewmate!"

"I understand," Sulu said, "but understanding doesn't carry weight. You have to be a Starfleet officer before you're anything else, Mr. Forester. Your bad judgment carries a price."

Drenched in shame, I glanced around at the crewmates I had doomed. What was next? My throat was dry, my voice cracked.

"Court-martial, sir?" I looked at him and Chekov. "If it's expulsion, sir, I'd like to point out that this was my idea, and my crew was only following orders."

"No cadet can order another cadet to break the law," Chekov pointed out.

A flickering chance exploded—he'd been ready for that one.

"We have something else in mind for your punishment," Sulu told me.

My eyes were almost adjusted. I could see his face, and the evil hint of a smile burrowing under there.

"We're moving up your simulation schedule. You'll have to face an advanced program, and deal with the scores as they come. If you do well, fine. If not, you'll be set back nearly a full semester's work. You'll have two days to prepare. At least your fate will be in your own hands. That's how we like it here."

I glanced at Chekov, then at Corin and Jana on one side, and Robin on the other. Chekov was passively mysterious. My crew was just scared.

Turning to Sulu again, I croaked, "I don't understand, sir."

"I know you don't," he said. "So here it is. In two days, ready or not, sink or swim, you and your crew will face the Kobayashi Maru No-Win Scenario on the main bridge simulator."

Commander Chekov folded his arms. "And may God have mercy on your souls."

Chapter 11

"I don't get it. What is this Maru thing?"

M'Giia's question threw me. Of course, she wouldn't know, being a communications specialist. Her world was a tapestry of frequencies and codes, acoustics, linguistics, and signals. Very technical, but didn't involve many decisions.

"It's a death sentence, that's what it is." I sat down between Robin and Jana in a secluded section of the lounge, well away from the main screen. "It's as impossible for us to break as the clue to who really blew up the lab. We can't beat it. The whole semester is ditched."

"Not very fair," Jana said. "They should either arrest us or clear us, but not this."

M'Giia frowned. "I still don't understand. What exactly is the Kobashi Scenario?"

"*Kobayashi*," I corrected. "The Kobayashi Maru. It's a simulator scenario that doesn't allow you to win.

I have no idea what the format is, but no matter what you do, the computer is programmed to countervail everything you try, and you eventually lose. How far you get into the program means something, and that's the trick, but you still lose. Not everybody has to face it. Only five percent of command cadet teams are made to face the No-Win Scenario. Usually, it's random. They've gotten some great commanders out of not-so-great cadets by tossing them into the No-Win and driving them just crazy enough to try things nobody in their right minds would try. But that's pretty rare. Generally, it's just a killer program, and you get set back. You go to the bottom of every Academy list and have to claw your way up all over again."

"But why would they do that to us!" M'Giia struck the couch cushion.

"Because it keeps the Academy's command school records clean for this year. No expulsions, no courts-martial. This is the command school's ninth year in a row without either of those. They want to make a decade."

"If no one's ever beat the Kobayashi Maru," Corin mourned, "then why even try?"

"So we don't go down in shame, that's why," Jana told him irritably.

"Well," I began slowly, "it's not exactly that no one's ever beaten it. One cadet did beat it."

"Who? When?"

"James T. Kirk. That's who. And when."

Corin gave Robin a victorious shove that almost knocked Robin off his chair. "Then it can be beat!"

M'Giia nodded. "If he could do it, so can we!"

I shook my head. "Nobody's done it since."

"Well, you know him, David," Jana said. "Maybe you can ask him how he did it."

"Oh, yes, Jana, and I'm sure he'll tell me if I just pay for the coffee. You've got to be kidding. We're not supposed to win. That's the lesson. Imagine asking James Kirk to help us cheat."

Corin reached across the table and shook my knee. "All we're asking is for a chance to beat the unbeatable! Come on—you're the best and the brightest, aren't you?"

"Oh, yeah, I glow in the dark."

"Hey, we've still got your command access code, remember?" Corin pointed out. "You haven't tried that yet. Maybe you can get through to the . . . something we could use."

"And don't forget, David," Jana added, "you could sift through the security database and see if there's any clue about whoever bombed the lab."

I looked at her. "How would the security database have that in it?"

"Well, somebody got in, right? Maybe they did what we did—used an access code to bypass security at the lab. You could see who's access codes were used to get into the lab in the hours just before the explosion."

"I'm sure the investigators have thought of that already, Jana."

"Maybe it'll mean more to you than to them. Maybe you'll think of something they didn't."

"That's it," Corin said. "Mission one, check the

security database. Mission two, find out how James Kirk beat the unbeatable. Cadet Forester, the future is yours!"

"You can do it, David!" M'Giia encouraged.

Robin just looked at me, his face a palette of doubt and worry.

"Well," I began, thinking, "I do still have to help Commander Chekov install—"

I cut myself off. The Klingon Heavy Cruiser was supposed to be classified. I knew that, yet I'd almost slipped. Had I come to trust these people that much? They seemed to trust me, even though we'd been caught in the lab, and I owed them something.

"All right," I said. "Sink or swim."

The non-security database could be shifted into classified with the command candidate's personal access code, and guess who had one? It meant we were trusted.

So much for trust.

I punched in my access code in lab Delta Foxtrot, which was being used as an alternate for Delta India, so there was no trouble hooking into the research Sturek had been doing.

But none of his conclusions were there. Only the unorganized details about metallurgy and residue that had been fed in from the fragments of those attack ships at Bicea. There was no proof here. Whatever Sturek had been referring to must've been on something portable, a Padd or a cartridge, probably for security reasons, destroyed in the explosion. The security had worked too well.

Security . . . and it hadn't worked well enough to keep a bomber from setting a trap. Had that person meant to get Sturek too? Or was that just an unfortunate bonus?

Yes, the investigators would check the lists of anyone who had used a command school access ID to get into the lab. So what? I could look too, couldn't I?

Maybe the names would mean something different to me than to a bunch of security grunts or elitist investigators.

Punch . . . pick . . . code . . . the list came up for the past six days.

The names were mostly instructors at the Academy, mostly science staff, and about a dozen command candidates, all team leaders and science officers. Nothing out of the ordinary.

Then I saw a name that made my heart jump. Robin Brady.

Why was Robin's name here?

To a security squad, Cadet Robin Brady was a command team engineer, with no red flags attached. They would pay no attention to his appearance on an access code to lab Delta India. An engineer could easily need to go in there.

Only to me, Robin's team leader, did this look out of place, and only because I knew Robin never had any reason to come into that lab. He and Sturek barely spoke and certainly weren't working together on the Bicea project.

I stared and stared at the name until it made me cold. Reason after reason came and went about why Robin might've come to Delta, but none stuck. After I ran out of reasons, I started inventing excuses, and those were even more flimsy.

Didn't make sense . . .

I ran the list again, and the second time through Robin's name seemed to flash at me again and again. Saboteur.

"Can't be," I mumbled, taking anchorage in the sound of my own voice. Why did it have to be so quiet in here?

A vital clue . . . but only to me. Was Robin's shyness hiding something that even I had never noticed?

"Crazy." I shook my head. There was just no reason. Not only no logical reason, but not even an illogical one either. Robin just wasn't the type to get involved with espionage. He got nervous at being late for a seminar.

But he was the only one here who wasn't a command team leader or a science officer. The only one. The only one . . .

"David?"

I bolted back from the computer terminal and almost toppled out of my chair. My hands slid on the console and knocked the data offline.

"Sir!" I choked.

Commander Chekov sauntered into the lab. "What? Did I frighten you?"

"I'm sorry, sir, it's just all this trouble with Sturek and the bomb—it's got me jumpy."

"Yes. Your friend is doing well enough, for a suspect," Chekov told me, and I couldn't tell whether or not he intended to make me feel better or worse.

"He had a mild concussion and has been under observation in his quarters. His communicator has been programmed to notify security if anyone discusses the incident with him, or anything about Bicea. So I recommend you don't try."

Oh, more good news. "No, sir, I won't try. I don't want to get him in any more trouble. Or any of us."

"Good." He handed me a set of computer cartridges and said, "Would you please load the Posnikoff series, sessions fourteen to forty-two, for the senior simulator runs of this coming week."

"Yes, sir . . . sir, aren't those really old missions?"

Chekov grinned. "As the wolf said to the songbird while devouring the old pheasant, 'Sometimes the oldest things are the tastiest.'"

He started away from me.

What was that supposed to mean? Just what I needed—something else that didn't make any sense.

"An ancient Russian folk tale," he tossed back over his shoulder as he situated himself at the master simulator inlet on the other side of the lab.

Well, that explained everything, didn't it? Old Russians again. No wonder they were old. Everybody else died of confusion trying to figure out their sayings.

Problems were piling up on me and I was feeling the weight. Sturek had to be cleared of suspicion. How did I know he was innocent?—good question. We hadn't been acquainted all that long, and there was more than just being crewmates. He might've blown himself up just to divert suspicion away from himself, but I couldn't believe he would blow me up too. He knew I'd just walked into the main lab. He could've waited until I was gone, or done it before, when he was alone. He hadn't shouted a warning, or even told me to take cover. If I pushed my imaginings, I could believe he might be a saboteur, but I didn't believe he was a murderer.

And Robin Brady had to be cleared too. He wasn't in trouble yet, but it was only a matter of time. Sooner or later, somebody in the investigation would find out he was the only orange in the basket of apples.

Both of these problems rode upon a bigger problem. In order to solve them, to clear my crewmates, I had to stay in the command school. My team had to remain a command team. If we were set back a semester, that meant being broken up and starting all over again, probably as crew in other command teams, and I wouldn't be selected as a team leader again. I'd be helm.

I couldn't let that happen. I had to stay at the command school, and remain team commander. And that meant only one thing—beating the Kobayashi Maru No-Win Scenario.

And there was only one person who knew how to do that.

I tried to be good, I really tried. No, I didn't. With the excuse of loading the Posnikoff series of maneuvers into the simulator computer, I was provided with a perfect excuse to dig through the ancillary programs regarding the No-Win test. There were no answers here, of course, since the test itself had encrypted into it over four hundred alternatives, all leading to failure. The program was ready for just about anything anyone could think of. And not even a command access code could get into that file, so I wasn't even tempted.

What did tempt me, I'm ashamed to say, was a personnel file with the name of the only cadet who had ever beaten the program. The private records of James T. Kirk.

"It can't be that easy," I muttered.

Could it?

As if unbidden by human mind, my fingers tapped in my command access code and keyed the Kirk file.

The screen scrolled merrily with information. Home: Riverside, Iowa. Father: Commander George S. Kirk, Starfleet Security Division. Missing in Action. Mother: Winona Kirk, Product Manager, Croughwell Corporation. Deceased. Siblings: George S. Kirk, Jr. Deceased.

"Another sole survivor," I murmured, and thought of M'Giia.

Then came the mission encapsulations—dozens of them. Omicron Delta, Gamma Trianguli, Neutral Zone, Triacus, the Gorn, the Horta, the Medusans ... scroll after scroll of missions and troubles and sacrifices. Even time travel, and he was still here to talk about it. To teach us about it.

I hungered for the time to read through all these missions and relive them, but not this way. These were just outlines, no details, no feelings, no conclusions. I wanted to read his logs from those days and really understand what he'd gone through and what made him so famous. He didn't seem like a hero in person, except for that little flash in his eyes.

And his words. When he talked to us about space . . . he was a hero then.

Kobayashi Maru.

I flinched. It appeared on the screen and my heart started fluttering.

Across the lab, Commander Chekov was involved with the other seventy-four maneuvers in the Posnikoff series and not paying attention to me. Good thing, because I was sure he could hear me sweat.

Perhaps he felt my eyes, for he chose that instant to glance at me. "Problem?"

"Uh . . . no, sir . . . just something tangling these codes. Some heavily encrypted data spliced onto the program for a mission."

"You shouldn't be playing with that."

How the hell did he know!

I clicked on the word *Kobayashi,* hoping to clear the screen before he tapped in, if he hadn't already, and up came another font, a mock-graffiti sprayed across the mission title.

"Tiberius was here."

The chair sunk under me because its pedestal melted. Next went my legs and after that my spine.

Chekov pushed away from his console and strolled over to sweep up the puddle with just my cerebral cortex sticking out like a straw.

"David . . . you're not supposed to be in that file."

My head rattled. I was nodding. "Do you want me to cancel it out, sir? I'll have to ask you to cross-cancel . . . the thing won't let me out."

"I know." He leaned on the top of my screen housing. "I froze the database."

Did he have the noose tied too? I looked up at him. "Why, sir?"

"Because I'm not the one who should decide whether or not you've breached privacy."

With a sinking stomach I watched as Chekov opened his communicator. "Chekov to Captain Kirk. Please join me in lab Delta Foxtrot right away."

"Hmmm . . . a little stroll down memory lane."

James Kirk's voice was mellow and unrevealing as he bent over my shoulder and looked at his own personal files.

"I'm sorry, sir," the only cadet in the room mourned pitifully. The only slime, the only slug, the only worm sweat.

"Sorry for what?" Kirk surveyed me with that sizzle in his eyes. "You're the only one who's ever had the nerve to look. It was right in there the whole time, and nobody else ever checked. Go ahead. Scroll the scenario. Won't get you anywhere."

Well, now it was an order. What could I say?—I don't want to, sir? Please don't make me?

I tapped the board.

The specs of the Kobayashi scenario ran before me. Nothing outlandish . . . a stranded Federation passenger freighter inside the Neutral Zone . . . no Starfleet ship allowed in there . . . atmospheric leakage . . . survivors begging for help. Seemed like any average program, except that this one wouldn't let the player win.

The player could choose not to go in, of course, but nobody did. A refusal to assist a ship in distress would be the blackest mark anybody could imagine on a performance record. We'd all learned that our first semester at the Academy.

Then the good stuff showed up. I peered at it with aching eyes, then turned in astonishment to Captain Kirk.

"You cheated!"

He gave me a little shrug and a nod. "Changed the rules of the game."

"But why?"

"Because there's no such thing as a no-win scenario. And I don't like to lose."

He crossed the room to a replicator and pulled up a cup of coffee. I pivoted in the seat and asked, "Isn't reprogramming the simulator against the rules?"

He didn't say anything, so I looked at Chekov and asked the same question silently this time.

Chekov raised his brows and refused to commit.

Kirk blew across the top of his cup of coffee. "After I beat the Kobayashi Maru, the administrators talked about tightening the rules, but they never did it. In fact, I got a commendation for original thinking. I learned to anticipate my enemy. Even if my enemy is just a computer."

There was something in there I should remember, but I couldn't make any sense of it. How could anybody anticipate an unknown?

Since I was in this deep anyway, might as well sink all the way.

"If you used this to cheat, then the Academy wouldn't be able to test how you handled a no-win scenario. Winning would be a foregone conclusion if you altered the programming in your favor."

"I didn't program it in my favor," Kirk said. "I didn't program a victory at all. I only made it possible to win. I still had to do the winning."

Chekov just leaned there on the counter, one hip up on the edge, his arms folded and one hand pressed to his mouth and behind that hand he was grinning at my expense. Oh, if there just weren't a rule against striking a senior officer . . .

"Forester," Kirk began, noticing that my attention had strayed just a hair.

"Sir?"

"I hear your science officer's under confinement. Has anyone in your crew been pushing you to get him out?"

He knew, and still he was making me say it.

"Well, yes, sir . . . "

"Good crew," he said. "You were faced with two choices. Gratify your crew by leading them in the wrong but popular action, or let them down by making an unpopular decision that left regulations intact."

That little break-in incident wasn't my favorite subject of conversation.

I gazed at the deck, at Captain Kirk's boots. "Yes, sir."

Kirk moved, just enough to make me raise my eyes. "Looks like you already faced a no-win scenario."

Was he congratulating me for breaking into the lab? Was there a senior officer in this place, on the grounds, or in space who could actually say exactly what he meant at any given moment?

This wasn't a time to be unsure. Was he going to make me guess?

"Do you want me to close the file down, sir?"

He sipped his coffee. "Suit yourself. And get my Klingon heavy cruiser working."

A simple nod to Chekov made the commander shove off the counter and fall in behind the captain as they both headed for the door.

"Captain," I called, pushing out of my seat—and I was pretty sure it left an impression on a key portion of my anatomy.

Kirk only half turned. "Question?"

"Which option did you choose? On the Kobayashi Maru."

He regarded me with the teasing amusement I'd never get used to, and then did what he did best— said nothing, and said it all.

"The winning one."

Chapter 12

"This is the *Kobayashi Maru*. We have struck a fission percussive mine . . . we have hull ruptures . . . position, Gamma Hydra, section 10. Life support systems failing—can you assist us, Lexington . . . can you assist us?"

"Data on the *Kobayashi Maru*, Mr. Sturek."

On the science monitor over Sturek's head, a raft of data scrolled out about a big ship, a cruising freighter.

"Crew of eighty-one," Sturek read off, boiling all the numbers down to what mattered. "Three hundred passengers."

I felt my brow crease. "Three hundred . . . "

"Life support is at critical failure . . . eighteen dead. Can you assist us!"

"Plot a course to the *Kobayashi Maru*."

I knew those words were expected of me, there was no way around them, but speaking them rubbed my throat raw. There was an option to abandon the crippled ship, but no cadet would ever take it. That would be an automatic loss. A negative score count.

"Course plotted," Jana said. Her voice was quaking.

"Take us in."

Corin nodded, but only once. "Helm's answering."

The starship around us seemed to swell . . . there was a difference about this program, a new feeling, new sounds. These weren't the sounds and sensations of a science vessel. The sounds were deeper, thicker, the bleeps and whirs more complex, the scanners brighter and more detailed. This was a starship.

"Warning: entering Neutral Zone."

"We're in violation of treaty, Captain," M'Giia informed, by the book.

"Red alert."

The whole bridge lighting scheme shifted slightly into the red, and our eyes adjusted.

"Shields up," I ordered. No point waiting until the last minute.

Was I anticipating? I had some idea of what was coming—conflict, battle, but no idea just what I'd be facing. Klingons, of course, but how many and in what formation?

I'd had my courses in maneuvering and battle strategy, I knew all the textbook moves and all the proper responses that would go down in my log as having done my best, the right thing at each point, yet somehow I wasn't reassured. This scenario, unlike most, wasn't designed to test what I had memorized. It was going for something completely else.

Before us on the big screen, the elliptical form of

the Neutral Zone was etched out in a grid pattern of red lines on the black curtain of space, with the entry point now behind us. In the middle of this big gap in Starfleet restricted space was one of the daring who crossed the Neutral Zone without protection, taking risks like this day's. The *Kobayashi Maru*, in distress.

"Captain!" Corin blurted suddenly. "Reading a Klingon warship fine on the port bow! Range, seventeen hundred kilometers. Reading a firing sequence!"

"Here we go," I muttered, then tossed over my shoulder, "Open hailing frequencies. Corin, weapons on line."

"On line, aye. David—Captain, two more ships," Corin rasped. "Approaching on a parabolic course, twenty-two thousand kilometers broad on the starboard stern."

Then he coughed slightly, as if the words had dried him out.

"Double shields astern," I ordered.

At the nav console Jana swallowed hard and tapped her board. "Double shields astern, aye."

Three ships. That changed everything. Any time more than one ship on any side entered a battle situation, there had to be organization. There had to be cooperation and method, patterns and plans. In my mind I ran through all the known Klingon techniques for a three-ship assault on one ship.

"Frequency open." M'Giia's voice was thready too. "They're hailing us, Captain—audio—"

"This is Captain Gorolock of the Klingon Empire. You are in violation of the Neutral Zone treaty. This is your trial. How do you plead?"

"This the *Starship Lexington.* We are on a rescue mission and have no hostile intent."

"Guilty as charged. Prepare to die."

Grasping the arms of the command chair, I stood up. I just couldn't stay in that chair very long. I just couldn't.

"Positions of the Klingon warships," I requested.

Corin glanced at his board. "They're all moving. Coming into some kind of spiral pattern around us. I think it's designed to keep us from turning without facing at least one ship."

On the screen, one of the warships swept past above us, and a few moments later a second one came by on the lower part of the screen. They were cooperating. If they decided to fire on us, which they would, they'd coordinate their firing sequences the way a boxer hits an opponent—to keep the wind driven out of us and never let us take a breath.

"Keep our shields to them as much as you can. M'Giia put him on visual."

My nervous anticipation started to sizzle into something else.

The screen flickered away from the view of the *Kobayashi Maru,* disabled, adrift on black sky, and provided a full-faced vision of a particularly slick-looking Klingon. Unlike most Klingons, this one had his hair tightly braided and draping across his ridged forehead and down to his shoulder plates. Dressed in polished leather body armor with brass bolts and clips, he was majestic and settled in his command status, not scraggly or brutish at all, like most

Klingons I'd seen pictures of, and I realized for the first time that I'd never seen a Klingon in person.

And this was designed to startle me, to bust the stereotype before I had a chance to take refuge in it. Worked.

Fine.

"Captain Gorolock," I greeted with a harsh tone, "Federation citizens are in immediate distress. There is no time to send for a civilian rescue ship. On my authority, Starfleet is taking charge of the rescue. As soon as we effect beaming of the passengers and crew on board, we'll evacuate the Neutral Zone. Stand down, or we will defend ourselves and the freighter to the fullest of our ability."

Gorolock's grand voice filled my bridge. "And who are you to dictate policy in the Neutral Zone?"

This was it. Now we'd see if I selected right.

"I am . . ."

Captain James T. Kirk.

"I am Captain David Forester."

On the wide vision of the Klingon bridge, Gorolock sat back in his chair, his eyes abruptly wide, and his mouth hanging open. Then, unexpected, his eyes lit up, his whole face took on a sheen of delight and joy.

"Forester!"

He stared and stared at me.

I blinked back like a stunned fish.

Now, I hadn't expected that reaction, that succulent, slurping astonishment. I'd expected something quite different—after all, I'd reprogrammed the simulator myself!

Cadet Kirk had found three choices when he reprogrammed the computer in his favor all those years ago. One, he could dumb down the Klingon artificial intelligence and make the captains fight clumsily, make mistakes, and miscalculate. Two, he could weaken their armaments and shields, just make everything less potent and the ships easier to beat. Three, he could program the simulator to make the Klingons respect and fear him personally. A pre-programmed reputation.

I had no idea which James Kirk had picked, but I'd gone for the third option—make the Klingon captains dread fighting the great David Forester. That way, I could keep a little of my self-respect. After all, how much respect could I cling to if I made the enemy weaker? If they feared me, this was only a psychological advantage. I'd still have to fight them, fullforce and outmaneuver them in open space.

But now, in this instant as I read Gorolock's vicious eyes and saw his posture change, and watched the faces of the Klingons on his bridge crew who came into the frame, my stomach sank and my skin began to shrivel. My blood went cold as I looked into Gorolock's unmasked delight.

I'd made a critical, blistering error. Much more than a simple mistake, I had completely underestimated my enemy. Instead of inflicting them with dread, I had just announced to a pack of rabid hounds, "Here I am, fresh red meat."

Gorolock leaned forward now, as if to push his elegant face into my bridge. His voice lowered to a hungry whisper.

"What a prize you shall be!"

Then he snapped something in Klingon at his bridge crew and the screen swept back to a view of space and the powerful warship churning past our bow.

Jana turned and looked at me, her face a mask of horror.

"Uh-oh . . . " Corin sat frozen to his controls, staring at the screen.

Drenched in the glue of my own miscalculation, I started shaking. Those weren't humans—why had I expected them to react like humans? I'd thought the reprogramming would make them hesitant to attack, might hold back, might even run.

Under the eyes of my crew, I gushed out a rough sigh. "Oh, God, I screwed up . . . "

"They're breaking formation," Corin gasped. "No pattern now—they're not taking any headings I can track! David, what should I do?"

"Uh—evasive maneuvers."

Was that the voice of a captain? That dull, muffled sound?

"Just what I always wanted," Corin sighed. "An exercise in futility. Why not?"

"They're firing!"

But the ship that fired on us wasn't the one directly in front of us—it was one of those at our stern. Not Gorolock's ship. What did that mean?

The bridge rocked and went a shade darker as the red alert lighting intensified and other lights flickered and went dark.

"Return fire," I said. What else?

Gorolock was the one who had contacted us, had spoken for the others, so why hadn't he been the first to fire?

My crew went about their jobs fatalistically now—I saw it in their movements, in their faces. They were trying to get the best scores they could in a losing situation. We'd had a chance of winning for just a flicker, then my mistake kicked in and we were facing the noose. My psychological advantage was shot to hell.

"Engineering," I asked over the hum of power-up, "can we throw a tow beam on the *Kobayashi Maru* while we fight?"

Robin's face was pale and sweaty. "Only by sacrificing firepower almost thirty percent."

"Don't do it."

"Acknowledged." He sounded relieved, but didn't look it.

"Emergency vector to heading four zero four, Corin."

Strange how calm my voice sounded. Was I fatalistic now too? Had I given up?

"They're all attacking!" Jana shouted. "All at once! Are they supposed to do that?"

"I thought there were attack patterns!" Corin said, struggling to maneuver through the sweeping warships as they looped past the main screen and were tracked by other screens around the bridge. The circle of screens gave us an idea of where those ships were in relation to the body of our starship, almost as if the monitors were windows. Of course, there weren't any in the ceiling or the deck, and from time to time the ships just disappeared, tracked only by the statistical data on other monitors. I had to keep my eyes in twenty places at once.

Of course, each sweep of each ship gave me an idea of where they were heading. "Jana, handle the phaser banks. Fire at will."

"Who's Will?" she mumbled, but she started shooting.

Phaser fire whined from our banks, shot upon shot, striking the enemy shields and skittering across the energy bubble, and were answered by shot after shot from the three Klingons, but not in any order. Their attacks had gone completely random.

"I've never heard of this," I uttered, trying to think as the bridge rattled and smoked around me. The smell of burning carpet and frying electrical connections made me dizzy, but somehow pared my thinking down.

Then I looked up.

"They're competing," I murmured. "They're ignoring each other! They're not working together!"

"Because they all want to be the one to capture the great you," Corin groaned, nearly choked by puffs of acrid smoke from his helm trunks.

"That's it!" I rushed forward to the helm, pausing between Jana and Corin, barely able to keep myself from trying to do their jobs.

But if I did theirs, I wouldn't be doing mine. And now I knew how to do that.

"Come about to six seven degrees true!"

"What? That'll put us right between two of them!"

"Do it, Corin!"

"All right, all right, sitting duck coming about—"

"Jana, plot a course down one third, straight down!"

She glanced at me. "You mean—"

"The numbers don't matter. Just be ready to move. They all want credit and they'll compete to get it. They were all working together till I told them who I was. Now it's a free-for-all. So we'll give them their chance. Go between them, Corin. Make us a target."

Corin fidgeted under my left elbow. "Coming between two of the warships . . . third one is veering in to block our path."

"Prepare to fire at all three warships at once."

His scorched face pivoted to me. "Are you kidding? That'll drain—"

I grabbed his shoulder. "I'm not kidding."

"Okay!"

"Fire!"

Three lancets of phaser fire broke from our banks and sizzled across the reduced shields of the three enemy ships, but divided by three the phaser energy was depleted—Corin was right about that—and couldn't bust through the remaining shields.

Then—and, boy, did I need something to go right—all three enemy ships opened fire from three sides of an imaginary triangle, all aimed at us, in the center.

"Engage evasive!" I shouted.

Corin hit his helm, Jana reenforced the gravitational holds on the ships inner structure to keep us from breaking apart, and the starship ducked into a horrible drop-off, as if we'd plunged from the top of a cliff.

The deck dropped out from under us. A sickening surge made my stomach heave and I fell. Above me on the upper deck, Sturek was thrown hard against his own console, and over there Robin came hurtling over the bridge rail to land beside me in a rolling heap.

On the main screen, a view of what lay above us, the three Klingons ships were caught in a spiderweb of each other's disruptor fire.

"Hah!" Corin came to his feet—how did he even find them?

"Sturek!" I grasped the command chair and hauled myself up. "Condition of those ships?"

Sturek pulled himself back to his sensor readouts and played the board with one hand—looked like the other was numb.

"All three ships scored direct hits," he reported. "Power ratios slipping . . . two ships completely disabled . . . engine power down to five percent . . . third ship is breaking up at the main structural joints. They are effecting abandon ship procedures." He turned, leaning hard on his board, and looked at me. "You did it, David."

The quiet avocation in his voice was like a fanfare on our smoky, smoldering bridge.

"David," M'Giia interrupted quietly from her post, "they're sending distress calls. They're completely disabled."

Why wasn't the program shutting down? Was there something else expected of me? I'd won, hadn't I?

"Prepare to retrieve escape pods and beam their survivors aboard. And ready a tractor beam for the

Kobayashi Maru. We'll tow it out of the Neutral Zone."

Well, why not? I had to keep going until the program shut down. Maybe the program wanted to see how many we could rescue—

Beep beep beep beep beep beep beep.

I swung around to the alert klaxon coming from the helm. "What?" I demanded.

"Another ship!" Corin brushed crumbs of insulation off his board and gawked at what he was seeing.

Then we saw it on the main screen too—another Klingon ship, but this one with four nacelles, a torpedolike body, and a main bulb as big as a whole Bird-of-Prey.

My voice tore through my gullet.

"The Klingon Heavy Cruiser! Damn you, Captain Kirk!"

Chapter 13

I stumbled up to the command platform and stared forward. "That's not supposed to be in this program! Damn it, damn it!"

Jana twisted around. "What are you talking about?"

"He did this to me on purpose. . . ! He re-reprogrammed the scenario!"

"Who? You mean Kirk?"

"Never mind! Shields double forward! I don't believe this is happening! Robin, tap the warp power for impulse maneuvering! I want the fastest changes you can give me. Phaser banks—"

"Their shields are triple power," Sturek reported. "At current strength, our phasers cannot disrupt them sufficiently to disable that ship."

"Will the photon torpedoes get through?"

"No way to be certain."

"Incoming!"

Corin's warning shout was swallowed by a hard burst from the Klingon Heavy Cruiser. The whole bridge surged up, then sideways, knocking the wind from us and blasting our bulkheads into fireworks. Half the engineering console blew up in Robin's face, driving him backward. This was no joke! Had anybody ever been killed in a simulator?

Robin stumbled into M'Giia, then recovered and slapped out a fire on the middle part of his controls. "Main engineering has taken a direct hit, Captain," he called over the noise. "Impulse maneuvering power is crippled."

"Another shot!" Corin grasped his helm to avoid being thrown out.

Didn't help. The heavy cruiser spat fire at us and we lurched. Jana and Corin both struck the deck an instant after I did, and for a horrible second we were tangled in each other's arms and legs. Then Corin found his center of balance and pulled me to my feet. I couldn't see Robin at all anymore, there was so much smoke boiling from the port side of the bridge. Ventilators hummed overhead, but they couldn't keep up.

"Aren't you going to shoot?" Jana demanded as she clawed back into her seat.

"You heard Sturek," I said. "We can't cut their shields with what we have left. Besides, why haven't they destroyed us? I know they could if they wanted to. So what do they really want? And why didn't those three ships cut us up while they had the chance?"

"What is this—twenty questions?" Corin complained.

"Maybe . . . I don't think anybody's ever gotten this far into the No-Win scenario, do you?"

Jana shrugged. "How would we know?"

"I don't," I told her. "But maybe they want something other than to destroy us."

"What are you going to do, then? Surrender?"

Oooh—that word crawled up my arms like a spider.

"Not a chance," I vowed. "I wouldn't give Kirk the satisfaction. He can expel me if he wants to. Full about! Ready photon torped—"

Shhhhhhh-Crack

"What's that?"

"Tractor beam," Sturek responded instantly. "High-resolution double-intensity energy cable. They've taken us in tow."

"Should I pull back?" Corin asked.

"No!"

He looked at me. "No?"

"No. Don't resist. That'll just drain us."

Sturek moved forward and stood over me on the upper bridge as we both looked at the main screen. "They're pulling us toward their side of the Neutral Zone."

On the screen before us, the four massive nacelles of the Klingon ship were turning toward us as the bow turned away, and we were captured. Not dead, but caught.

They didn't destroy us. Was their mission to capture a starship? Was that it?

How many cadets had run from the onslaught of Klingon ships, assuming their intent was to destroy?

I held my breath a moment, partly because the smoke was making me sick, and partly because I was waiting for the program to declare me a loser and shut the simulator down.

But it didn't. We just stayed in tow, watching ourselves being pulled into Klingon space.

Robin staggered out of the port side smoke. "Why isn't the program shutting down? We're caught, aren't we?"

With one hand on the back of Jana's chair, I pulled myself to the command platform. "Yes, we're caught . . . but maybe there are still more options."

"What options?" Corin asked. "We can't hurt that tank with phasers. You still want to try the torpedoes?"

"No . . . that'd be too easy. I don't think that's it."

Moving behind Corin so I could see his readouts, I watched the big ship on the screen, and the disabled Klingon ships we'd left floating around us, right where they'd shattered each other. Two of them were flanking our path. The heavy cruiser would pull us right between them.

"No propulsion," I murmured, thinking aloud, "phaser power is diminished, photons unreliable, enemy triple-shielded . . . under tow . . . no warp power . . . hold it—that's it."

"What's it?" Jana asked, and there was a glint of hope in her voice. Were they starting to have a little faith in me?

Even the illusion gave me strength.

"Warp power," I said, slipping into the command chair. My legs tense, I couldn't make myself settle back, but I wanted something to hold on to, so I grasped the arms of the chair as if holding a horse's reins. "Jana, target photon torpedoes on the derelict Klingon warship coming up on our port bow."

"Why? They're done for!"

"Yes, and that's why. Robin, flush all weapons power into one concentrated phaser. Prepare to fire point-blank on my mark."

Her console fritzed and complained, but evidently responded, because she said, "Phasers armed and ready. We'll only have one burst at this level of power concentration."

"Understood . . . ready . . . "

The derelict Klingon ship floating with one nacelle down, like an ornament on a string as we approached. The Klingon Heavy Cruiser would reach and pass it first. That was the moment I wanted.

A few more seconds . . . they were almost abeam of each other.

"Brace yourselves," I said. "Robin, hold on."

Bruised and scorched, he flinched at the sound of his name, but broke his trance and got a grip on the rail.

Two more seconds . . . one . . .

"Fire!"

Chapter 14

Jana hunched to her controls. On the main screen, bulbs of blue light blew from our ports and lanced into space, not toward the heavy cruiser, but at the damaged Klingon warship off our port bow.

The warship lurched hideously as the phasers struck its underbelly—dead hit, right in the warp core.

"Direct hit," Sturek reported. "Warp reaction is—"

The screen erupted into a brilliant white plume with Easter sparkles dashing toward us—bits of incendiary matter instantly liquefied by the colossal explosion of a warp engine ripping itself inside out. Big enough to take out a planet, the detonation instantly engulfed the heavy cruiser, snapped the tractor power, jolting us free of the pull, then swept over us like a tidal wave.

The bridge rolled beneath us and half the forward

wall came caving in, and the main screen was torn almost in half on a jagged angle. Now, that was something I'd sure never seen before.

"It worked!" Corin clung with both hands to his helm. "If we'd been under propulsion, we'd have been crushed! David, that's great!"

Actually, I hadn't thought of that. What luck. By not resisting the heavy cruiser's tractor beam, we weren't under any thrust, and that allowed us to ride the concussive wave like a surfboard instead of being smashed as if we'd hit a wall.

"Ship's condition?"

Robin's choking from the upper deck twisted into words. "Engines . . . off line . . . impulse drive is under repair . . . shields down to ten percent . . . "

"Minimal helm capacity," Corin reported. "Some thruster power available on aft and starboard thrusters."

"Weapons still online, but power's reduced two thirds," Jana said, and she was grinning.

"Life support stable," Sturek murmured, barely audible as we watched the Klingon Heavy Cruiser grind and tumble on the working half of the screen. Then he looked at his sensor panel. "Heavy cruiser sustained considerable damage . . . three of the four nacelles as out of alignment. Their propulsion system is compromised. They're adrift."

"So are we," I said. "It's a draw. I guess that's the best we'll get. Sorry, guys."

"Program shut-down," the computer voice finally came, both a shock and a relief. "Your ship is adrift.

You have cast your enemies adrift. Your scores will be posted at zero nine hundred hours."

My hands were tingling. One of my legs ached—and I wasn't even sure which one . . . left one. Knee. My face felt hot, wet. My crew looked as if they'd been shot through the business end of a phaser rifle.

"You did great, David," Corin murmured, turning to me. "I never thought anybody could get this far."

I tried to respond, but could only manage a nod.

"At least we know you'll fight," M'Giia offered with a warm glow of approval.

"I'll never doubt you again," Jana added.

On the engineering deck, Robin drew heavy breath after heavy breath and smiled at me, and Sturek came down to stand at my side. Their silent testimonials were almost too much to bear.

"You all did great," I managed. "Better than ever. You're turning into a crew."

How they felt about that, I couldn't tell. There was no way to say it any better, so I just turned to Sturek and offered a hand.

He took mine, and his eyes smiled.

"All right, open 'er up."

The voice came from behind the smoke, inside the whir of fake damage, and all around us the engine sounds began to shut down.

It was over, it was over. No win.

The panels parted beside the destroyed viewscreen. There, enshrouded in whispering smoke and crowned by sparks still drifting from the ceiling, Captain James Kirk strolled onto the bridge from a place where in real life there wouldn't even been a door. At his sides were Captain Sulu and Commander Chekov, followed by about a dozen technicians, advisers, and clean-up artists.

Full complement. I braced to take what was coming.

Kirk strode across the upper deck. Sulu and Chekov lagged back, looking around at the level of damage wrought by our persistence. Their amusement was irritating.

"Everyone all right?" Kirk asked. Damn him, he thought all this was funny.

Robin managed a nod, then stepped out of his way.

No one else in my crew made any response to him. It was as if we'd been boarded.

Then I realized something else was happening that never had before—they were letting me speak for them.

"We're fine, sir," I said, even though I didn't know for sure.

He stepped down to my level. "Your lip's bleeding."

I didn't wipe it. "Yes, sir."

"Quite a mess here," he said, glancing around. "You've achieved a level never before matched by any cadet in the Kobayashi Maru test."

Anguished, I ground out a miserable, "Thank you, sir. But we didn't save the freighter, and we lost the battle."

"You weren't captured," he told me, holding up a finger. "That was the actual goal of the Klingons. By rendering all ships derelict, even your own, you prevented a starship from falling into enemy hands. Technically, you've just effected a win."

"Yes!" Corin jumped up and clapped me on the back.

Somebody else grabbed me in a body hug from my right and for a crazy moment I thought it was Sturek, but it turned out to be Jana.

Then James Kirk held his hand out to me. "Mr. Forester, you've just become the second cadet to beat the No-Win Scenario. Congratulations to you, and to your crew."

All around, the officers, technicians, advisers, and other cadets broke into applause.

I just stood there, my sore knee trembling, my left hand gripping the arm of the command chair to keep me on my feet. Somehow I couldn't feel deserving of all this. I'd cheated, and it had backfired. So I handled it well and got lucky—so what?

After a few more pats on the back and handshakes, the bridge fell to a busy murmur as technicians crawled around, shutting off power to the snapping circuits and sparking ruptures.

"Now," Kirk said, "Captain Sulu?"

"Yes." Sulu stepped forward. "Cadet Forester, report to the commandant's office for reprimand."

"Reprimand?" Corin blurted.

"There's still the problem of having reprogrammed the simulator, and the issue of breaking and entering. The rest of you are confined to quarters until further notice. Dismissed."

Chapter 15

"Why did you cheat?"

Commandant Rotherot sat behind his desk like some kind of overfed inquisitional barrister. I stood before him, and Sulu and Chekov were in the office too, with Sulu leaning against a wall with his arms folded, and Chekov sitting on the leather couch.

I'd expected Captain Kirk to be here too, but I guess he was sparing me the embarrassment. Gee, thanks.

"The simulator shows evidence of tampering," Rotherot went on, without waiting for an answer to his first question. "What've you got to say for yourself?"

What could I say? That changing the parameters of a simulation isn't exactly cheating by a strict reading of the rules? How would that sound? That I wanted to impress my crew? That I needed to beat the No-Win in order to stay in command school long enough to clear my science officer of sabotage and my engineer of espionage?

"So my ship could survive, sir," I said. Good as any.

"Reprogramming the simulator may not violate the letter of the law," he said, "but it's a violation of everything we've been trying to teach you. Therefore, we've decided to take disciplinary action against you."

My spine went rigid, and I actually leaned forward an inch. "That's not what you did to Cadet Kirk, sir!"

"The Academy can take any disciplinary action it chooses," Captain Sulu said. "We're putting you on probation and letting it be known that we're considering expulsion."

I parted my lips to protest, then decided that just wouldn't help. What about Sturek? And Robin?

"Don't worry, David," Chekov said. "How good would it look for the Academy to expel the second cadet to ever beat the No-Win test?"

"So you're not going to expel me?"

Was the room spinning?

"No," Sulu said. "We just want things to appear that way. So you appear desperate."

I licked my cut lip. "Sir . . . I don't understand."

"Cadet," Rotherot began, "what would you be prepared to do in order to clear your science officer of the bombing charges?"

Facing him, I blurted, "Anything, sir!"

"Good," Sulu said. "We believe Cadet Sturek is innocent. However, there's evidence to indicate that another of your crew may have been involved in the incident."

My chest felt as if it were caving in. They knew.

"Yes, sir," I admitted with a sinking tone. "Robin Brady."

"If you had evidence," Rotherot charged, "you should've brought it to our attention immediately!"

"I stumbled across it just before taking the Kobayashi Maru. I did know how to handle it. So I decided to keep it to myself until I could confront him as his commanding officer."

Sulu nodded approvingly. He seemed to understand better than Rotherot did. "Cadet Brady is confirmed as being in the engineering library at the time his access codes were used to break into the lab. We don't believe he's the one who set the bomb."

"I never believed it either, sir," I told him with a rush of relief.

"To find out who did," he went on, "we'd like you to undertake a covert mission for us."

Rotherot stood up and came around his desk. "We'll announce that you're on probation. We'll tell the cadets that we found some vital clue as to the identity of the bomber and that we're examining it in the science lab compound analysis section."

Chekov stood up too. Were we going to dance?

"Then," the commander said, "you get to complain about how unfairly the Academy has treated you. Hint that you're looking for a way to get back at us. A lot of the cadets know you've been working with me on the simulators, and that you have access to the lab."

More relaxed now, Rotherot held up a finger. "Now, keep in mind, Cadet—if you agree to assist us, you cannot talk about this mission to your team. They must believe you're being expelled."

"Well?" Sulu asked. "Are you ready to take on the challenge?"

They squared off in front of me, and they already knew my answer. Great, because it was a complete surprise to me when it came out.

"Yes, sir. I'm ready."

"Congratulations," Sulu said with a canny smile. "You're officially on probation pending expulsion from Starfleet Academy. Good luck with your mission. And don't forget—this one's no simulation. Dismissed."

The cadets' lounge was a flurry of mixed emotions awaiting me from two dozen fronts. My own crew sat in a corner clutch of chairs, their faces in the carpet, and between us was a field of cadets, some sullen, others beaming.

I was pummeled with congratulations and sympathy as I tried to get through to my crewmates. Some people lauded me for beating the No-Win, and others expressed anger or regret that I was being expelled. I felt as if I were the star attraction at a funeral— people mourning and murmuring reassurances at the same time.

Finally I broke through all the handshakes and backslaps and attempts at moral support, and joined my crew in the corner. Sturek, of course, was conspicuously missing, still in confinement since he hadn't been cleared. Yet.

"We have to do something," M'Giia said instantly. No hello, no nothing. Just that.

"We can't just let them expel you, David," Jana agreed. "We've all agreed to stand up for you. If they want to expel you, they'll have to explain to all of Starfleet how they expelled an entire command team."

Corin squeezed my arm. "Right."

Robin handed me a hot cup of something—chocolate—and I turned to him with a sad smile. I was glad to see him and be free of the suspicion. "I'm not about to get the rest of you expelled trying to help me," I told them. "We tried to help Sturek, and it backfired. We're not trying that again. I've got my own plans."

"What does that mean?" Robin asked.

"Hey, Forester." It was Frank Malan. He came through the lounge with three of his own crewmates, not looking very sympathetic. "Well, well, well . . . guess you're a civilian again, right?"

Corin vaulted to his feet and rammed Malan back into two of his crewmates. "You're about a milli-second from sudden death, Malan!"

"Corin!" I jumped up and pulled him back. "Settle down."

Luckily, he'd gotten to like taking orders from me.

Turning to Malan, I simply requested, "Get the hell out of here, Frank."

"He's looking for a fight," Jana accused.

"No, he's not," I said. "He knows there isn't one here. Right, Frank?"

"Oh, right," Malan mocked. "Sure knew that. Didn't mean to break up your pity party."

With a victorious glance at his crew, he gave me an unconvincing pat on the shoulder and vectored off.

"Everybody sit down." I settled back onto the couch next to M'Giia.

Corin could only manage to perch on the arm of Robin's chair. "I still think we should take some action. Confiscate the scores or the files or burn down a building or something. If the evidence against you disappeared, what could they do?"

I smiled. What an idea.

"This is unjust!" M'Giia agreed. "The Academy is wrong!"

"It's my fight," I told them. "I want all of you to stay out of it. I haven't been expelled yet. I'm just on probation."

"Pending expulsion," Robin reminded me. "It's not fair, David."

"Yes, it is," I said.

Just when I was trying to think up a great lie for which they might not hate me later, Cadet Faith Gage appeared in front of me.

Faith Gage. Just the person I wanted to see. Corin had wanted to be attractive to her, Robin had wanted to, and suddenly I wanted to.

"Hello, David," she said then. "Can I speak to you for a minute?"

"Oh, sure." I looked at my crewmates. "You guys better get going. Believe it or not, we have another simulator mission at eight hundred hours. Better get some rest."

They didn't want to leave me, and that made me feel better. On the other hand, I hoped they would just go. The less time I spent with them, the less I had to keep from telling them the truth. I'd just won their trust, and now it had to be risked.

"Go on," I encouraged, in a tone that was meant to communicate that I was okay, not upset, resigned to fate, could be left here, wouldn't jump off Golden Gate Bridge.

Faith Gage was sympathetic enough to offer Robin a hug on his way past me, but there was something hollow and superficial about it. I couldn't tell whether or not Robin got that feeling. Soon I was sitting alone with her, and the other cadets in the lounge were making a point of not coming around.

"David," she said again, "I heard about what the command staff did to you. They're completely unfair."

"I know."

"Look, David, I know time might be short, so I've got to tell you . . . I visited Robin the day before the explosion. I spotted a schematic for a homemade bomb in his quarters."

I tried to keep any reaction out of my face, but I don't think I succeeded. "You think Robin planted the bomb?"

"I don't know! But when I heard they found some new evidence, I was worried."

"That's good of you, Faith." I patted her hand, hoping the move wasn't too ridiculous. "You're the only friend Robin has, outside of our team. You're the only person he's talked to since we got to command school."

"Oh, I know," she said. "I don't want to see anything happen to Robin."

"Neither do I. But what can we do about it?"

She put her long, elegant fingers across my arm. "I'm afraid he was driven to this by his infatuation with me . . . I feel responsible. David, if they're going to expel you anyway, then I'm the only one with anything to lose. You've still got the access code. And I know where to look for the evidence."

I was either the luckiest bastard in Starfleet or the unluckiest. What a target I made.

"Where?" I asked.

"In the lab," she said. "If there are any remnants of the things I saw in Robin's quarters, we can get them out of there before the investigators find them."

"But if Robin's guilty," I suggested, "he should get caught, shouldn't he?"

"I think it's my fault," she said quickly. "Whatever he's involved in, it's got to be just to get my attention. Somebody's using him. I'm willing to risk breaking in, if you'll go in again. I've only got a communications access code. The lab security system requires command or engineering."

Keeping my voice low, I nodded. "Why not? They can't expel me twice, can they?"

"Good." She smiled. "Okay, I'll meet you tonight, after the nebula analysis seminar."

"Perfect."

* * *

"Can you get me into the computer?" Faith asked.

"Sure."

"You look nervous, David. You want to help Robin, don't you?"

"I'm just a little jumpy lately. Don't worry about me, Faith, just do what you can."

"Type in your access code."

The lab computer made no sounds, but flashed bright patterns on Faith Gage's classical features as we huddled in the darkened room. I didn't know why she wanted to be here, but it sure wasn't to clear Robin Brady.

It bothered me a little that she thought I was so dense, but maybe she had that power over people. She certainly had it over Robin, and shy or not, he wasn't stupid.

"Look at this," she said. "Robin used his access code the day of the break-in. It looks like the investigators stored the remains of the bomb in locker D-forty-seven."

"Let's take a look."

She was too eager. She pushed out of the computer chair and hurried to the security lockers around the corner. I was the only one here who could access the locker code. She could've easily just let me do it by myself, but instead she crowded me at the locker panel like a hungry wolf.

I keyed my command candidate code, and the locker's magnetic trap clicked. The panel slid open.

Faith nudged me aside and looked in. "There's nothing in here!"

Her voice changed to a bitter snarl—no more seduction in it at all. She backed away and drew a concealed palm phaser.

"What's going on, David!"

I lowered my chin and glared at her. My nervousness fell away. Now I was just angry. "What are you doing, Faith?"

"Just stay over there!" She glanced around. "This is a trap!"

"You used Robin's crush on you to get the code from him," I said.

Her pretty face crumpled with fury and misery. "How did you know? Even the investigators didn't know!"

"Because I know Robin better than the investigators do. He hardly ever speaks to anybody except our crew, and you were the only person who had any effect on him. He even did what you said and went to the Vanguard meetings. That's a pretty powerful spell you cast on him. And you planted the bomb that almost killed Sturek. Why, Faith? What makes a cadet do something like that?"

Her complexion paled. "We never meant it to go this far. But we couldn't let Sturek finish his project! We had to be sure the Klingons got blamed for Bicea!"

"Who's 'we'?"

"You can still work with us, David! You can still join the Vanguard!"

"Vanguard," I sighed. Again. I guess I knew, not all that deep down.

"You're just the right kind of person for us," she encouraged. "You could join us and stand at Captain

Kirk's side as the only two people to ever beat the No-Win scenario!"

I took a ridiculous step toward her, and toward that phaser, and her posture suddenly changed enough to show me that she'd use the weapon if I didn't back off. "What's Captain Kirk got to do with the Vanguard?"

"He's our hero," she said with quiet awe. "We're approaching him to be our leader."

"Are you kidding? James Kirk?"

"David, he hates Klingons. They killed his son. Don't you know that?"

"No, I didn't know that . . . "

"If we could get him on our side, we can change Federation policy toward Klingons and all the other hostile races out there. We could aggressively end their reign of terror over whole sectors of the galaxy. Think of how life would improve!"

My chest started to hurt and I realized I'd stopped breathing. So I breathed. And got a headache.

"Faith . . . you guys really believe in all this, don't you?"

"Yes! I'm sorry about Sturek. He wasn't supposed to be caught in the explosion. It was just bad timing. It's about the survival of the Federation, David!"

Inner rage boiled up in me for the inexcusable mistake that almost cost my crewman's life.

"Well, I hope this was worth ruining your career, Faith," I said. "You're under arrest."

Her face hardened. "I've got the phaser, David. I'm going to kill you and leave your body next to the empty locker. I'll tell them you committed suicide when you couldn't find the evidence."

"That won't hold up."

"I think it will. I've got ways of making people trust me."

"I know you do. There's just one problem."

Her lovely eyes narrowed. "What problem?"

Tremendous relief flushed over me when Captain Sulu, Commandant Rotherot, and three security guards stepped out of the auxiliary lab, all three holding phasers on Faith Gage.

"It's not his trap," Sulu said.

For an instant, through the shock on Faith's expression, I saw her hand cramp briefly on the phaser that was aimed at me. Then the terrible doubt caught her by the throat and she couldn't go through with killing me. I wanted to believe there was pure humanity at work in her, but had to live with the disappointment that she was just looking out for herself. An espionage charge was less grave than a murder charge.

"Looks like we caught our bomber," Rotherot said. "Good work, Cadet Forester."

As he and Sulu came to my side and the security guards took charge of Faith, I leaned against the locker and said, "Strange . . . I thought it would be Frank Malan. Guess I misjudged him."

"It happens," Sulu said with a grin. Then he turned toward the auxiliary lab and called, "Cadet Sturek, come out, please."

Now, I hadn't expected this, but here came Sturek. I guess they wanted him to see how far I'd gone to clear him. I looked at Sulu with tremendous gratitude as Sturek came to my side.

"I appreciate your standing by me, David," he said sincerely. "I have never before enjoyed such devotion."

Offering only a smile, I backed it up with a handshake and a feeling we both shared of how good it was to stand together.

"Cadet Forester," Rotherot began with that puffed-up pomposity he did so well, "your actions were above and beyond the call of duty. Any charges against you are hereby dropped and you are fully reinstated at Starfleet Academy. You have the appreciation of the entire command staff of Starfleet Academy."

What could I say?

"I'm honored to serve, sir."

Not bad.

"Cadet Sturek," Rotherot went on, "it's my pleasure to clear you of any suspicion of sabotage, and you may continue your work on the Bicea attack ship. Cadet Forester, we would like you to assist Mr. Sturek in his analysis."

"Sir?"

"And also, we would like you to help us investigate the further activities of the Vanguard. Will you do this?"

I gazed at him briefly, then at Sulu, who said, "It's not official business, David. You're free to decline."

Oh, sure.

"I'd be happy to assist, sir."

"Good. Then you need to be brought in on the secret about Sturek's work and why the Vanguard thought they had to destroy the evidence. Tell him, Mr. Sturek."

I turned to my science officer. Sturek looked drawn and overworked, but relaxed and relieved that he'd been cleared of suspicion. "I found a neural network etched into the molecules of the attack ship."

"What does that mean?" I asked.

"It means the ship itself is a life-form."

"You're kidding! A ship that's alive? You mean a life-form that just looks like a ship?"

"In some manner, yes. Or a vessel that is tied directly into the living bodily functions of those who drive it."

"It also means," Sulu added, "that the Klingons had nothing to do with the massacre on Bicea. They have no technology like that."

"Sir," I began, "if Sturek's evidence was destroyed in the bombing, how can we keep going with the investigation and prove it wasn't the Klingons?"

Sturek offered a subtle Vulcan version of a shrug. "I memorized some of the DNA sequences and metallurgical compounds and have fed them back into a database. They're incomplete without the actual fragments and molecular structure. Identification will be painstaking, but there's still a chance of breaking the genetic code and discovering who is staging these attacks. The work will not be easy, David. You should reconsider."

"No, I'm not going to reconsider. I'm going to help stop whoever's doing these things. Just for M'Giia's sake if nothing else."

"Whoever it is," Rotherot said, "they've got mass

murder to answer for. We can't have this in the galaxy."

"No, sir," I agreed. "We can't."

"Congratulations, Cadets," Sulu said, with that quizzical you're-in-trouble-now gleam in his eyes. "Now you get to do the really hard work."

Chapter 16

"Sturek, you're overworking yourself."

"Vulcans have excellent stamina."

"You're neglecting your training too. It's not your fault that the proof was lost. If anything, it was my fault. I should've gone into that fire and pulled your data out."

"You'd have been killed, David."

"And thousands of innocent people are being killed in these random attacks. If I'd taken action in the lab, we might've stopped these massacres by now."

"You'd have been killed."

For days our lives had been a pattern of work and training overlaid by more work. I hadn't had more than four hours' sleep a night for nearly a week. We still had our simulator obligations, our physical training, our drilling, enough to keep up the appearance of being ordinary cadets who weren't working on anything special for Starfleet. Of course, our crew noticed, and that meant word got around that something was going on.

If I was overworking myself, Sturek was virtually committing suicide. He didn't sleep at all. He just kept digging and analyzing and recalibrating the scraps of data he'd stored in his mind after the explosion. For every ten feet we climbed, we'd slip back eight.

But as much as we were suffering, there were others who were suffering more. M'Giia, who had lost her entire family. The thousands of victims in the border colonies and outposts who had been killed or injured, who had lost loved ones, and who were scrambling to defend themselves against the expected unknown.

I found it dazzling that Sturek and I might be the only things standing between those people and more destruction. We felt so isolated here . . . .

And the real torture was that we really weren't getting anywhere. Days of work with very little to show for it. We were climbing an ice ladder.

Around noon on the fifth day, I gave up.

"Sturek, we're stumped. We've got to admit to Captain Sulu that we just don't have enough to work with here."

He turned to me, and I could see that he wanted to argue, to tell me that this was Starfleet, duty, honor, "give up" wasn't in our vocabulary, but the frustration was in his eyes too. His face was grooved by exhaustion.

"I'm forced to agree," he said with terrible reluctance. "Is there nothing we can do?"

I started to say no, but I couldn't make it come out.

I was his commanding officer. He expected more from me. *I* expected more from me. There had to be something—

"I'll resign from the command school," I said abruptly. "I'll volunteer for a recon mission to Bicea or one of the other attack sites and gather more fragments."

"That could take months," Sturek pointed out.

I started to respond, but another voice cut through the room. "It won't take months."

We both turned as Captain Kirk strode briskly toward us, carrying two handfuls of scorched metal.

"Captain!" I gasped. "I thought you'd shipped out, sir!"

"I did. But there was another attack along the Klingon Neutral Zone three days ago." He tossed the metallic shards onto the table where Sturek and I were working. "Fragments of the attacking vessel, sheared off by planetary defense. They've got the same etchings that Sturek discovered before. Since you did the initial analysis, I persuaded Starfleet to turn the fragments over to you. We're back in business."

So he was one step ahead of me all the way. What a surprise.

"I know we're asking you to jeopardize your training," Kirk went on, "and I'm not here to tell you how to spend your time. I'm here to extend an opportunity. You two are being given command responsibility. Whether you take it or not, it's up to you."

Feeling the pressure of innocent lives on our hands, I looked at Sturek. He nodded.

I picked up one of the fragments and looked at Captain Kirk. "We'll figure it out, sir."

His eyes got that dangerous twinkle. "Yes, I think you will."

He turned on a heel and strode out, and was met at the door panels by M'Giia, who stepped aside for Captain Kirk to pass. The captain nodded a greeting at her, but made no other comment or indication that he knew anything about her—and he did, of course.

I got a very clear message from that subtle lack of attention—he was leaving her to me.

"David . . . " M'Giia began as she came into the lab, "you wanted to see me?"

Sturek picked up one of the fragments and politely turned his back, heading over to the spectral analysis chamber and leaving the two of us alone.

"Yes," I said to her. "M'Giia, are you a member of the Vanguard?"

She looked startled, then embarrassed.

"I know you've been to their meetings," I added.

Then she nodded. "It was for your own protection, David."

"My protection? What's that supposed to mean?"

"After the attack on Bicea, I did go to their meetings. I was angry and Frank Malan had answers I wanted to hear. But then Faith tried to frame Robin. I couldn't stand for that. And since the Klingons have been moving more toward peace with the Federation, the Vanguard's starting to talk about violent action."

"What's that got to do with protecting me?"

"Some of the Vanguard want you to join them.

They were impressed when you beat the Kobayashi Maru, and they think you're 'their type,' whatever that is. They know James Kirk likes you, and they think Kirk's on their side."

"Because of his attitude about Klingons . . . I get it."

"He hates them and everybody knows it. And the Klingons hate him right back. I stayed in the Vanguard because I wanted to hear what they were saying about you."

I lowered myself onto a stool and tried to clear my head. "Do you have any proof that the Vanguard is going to get violent? Have you mentioned this to Captain Sulu?"

"Yes, I did. But his official policy is hands off the Vanguard to avoid making them into martyrs. He's going to wait for them to do something really illegal before moving in. I don't have any proof to back up what I think. They let me in, but they're very guarded. They only trust humans."

We fell silent for a few moments, hearing only the click and scrape of Sturek as he plunged into analysis of the new fragments in the other room. The problem with waiting for the Vanguard to do something illegal was that somebody could get killed. Having come so close to losing Sturek, I couldn't summon up that much patience.

"Well . . . if they think I should join them . . . maybe I should."

M'Giia frowned. "You mean . . . infiltrate? David, you can't fool them. They've got a telepath who clears everybody at the door. You'd have to think like them. And I know you don't."

"Is this telepath human?"

"Yes, she is. She trained someplace other than Earth, though."

"Human telepaths aren't that reliable," I said. "But Vulcans are."

Her eyes widened. "Sturek! Of course! He could use a mind meld to mask your thoughts! You could pretend you found a cover-up that turned you against the Federation!"

"You have an evil mind, M'Giia," I said. "I like it. But mind meld have to wait until Sturek and I get a handle on this cybership project. Lives are at stake."

"What do you want me to do?" she asked.

"You . . . keep going to the Vanguard meetings. Keep your ears open. Report to me if you hear anything other than hot propaganda."

"I understand," she said. "There's a meeting in half an hour. I wasn't going to go . . . but I will now."

"I'll be in navigation class with the rest of the crew if you need me. M'Giia, be careful. Frank Malan and his kind aren't the trusting types."

"You'll be required to memorize combinations of long-range visual signals that signify hundreds of ship's conditions. Under power, not under power, adrift, in distress, under tow, embarking, personnel in spacewalk, keep your distance, vessel damaged, stop immediately, warning, require assistance, veering starboard or port, in reverse, wish to communicate . . . and many others. You must be able to recognize these visuals instantly in half-second flashes. Any questions?"

"Yes, sir," one of the helm candidates asked. "Why are visual signals necessary? With available communication technology, we'll know the condition of any ship before we ever come within visual range in open space."

"Good question." Commander Chekov looked up from the mass of laminated charts Captain Kirk had left behind on the big table in the navigation seminar hall. "Any answers?"

"Comm link failure," Robin Brady automatically said as he stood just behind my left shoulder.

"Subspace interference," someone else suggested.

Another cadet added, "Spatial distortion."

"Anything else?" Chekov eyed us, implying that there were plenty of others and he wasn't satisfied, and he wasn't going to help.

"The crew could be sick or unconscious," I suggested.

"Ah!" He held up a hand. "Never forget there could be a non-technical answer. Very good, Mr. Forester."

From behind Corin clasped my shoulders and gave me a congratulatory shake. As exhausted as I was, I found myself particularly grateful and burdened by their pride. My crew had been enjoying the reputation of competitive spirit since we beat the No-Win, and the reputation was getting harder and harder for me to live up to. And the salty jealousy of the other cadets was something I hadn't anticipated.

"Get out! Get out of the room!"

The desperate call came from the main entrance. Like a flock of lemmings we all turned and gawked.

It was M'Giia!

She came charging into the room, between the rows of seats toward the lecture area and the display table where we were all clustered.

"Do what she says!" I shouted spontaneously. I spun around and shoved Corin and another cadet away from the table.

The other cadets, naturally, turned to Commander Chekov, but he was no fool. He grabbed two cadets near him and veered them into movement.

"Do it!" he shouted, and began herding the cadets toward the nearest lecture-level exit.

M'Giia came down the center isle, calling, "Hurry! Get out! Everyone—"

I glanced over my shoulder at the cadets who were still too stunned to move, and angled back to shove some of them along. Skidding along the rim of the table, I grabbed Robin Brady, who was completely dumbfounded.

"Robin, move!"

I hauled on his arm like a tug-of-rope, but in a fit of panic he resisted for a crucial instant before letting me move him.

Overhead there was a ghastly crack—and the ceiling caved in!

Chapter 17

Structural members as big around as my shoulders came crashing onto the table, and the table buckled. Ceiling material, bricks, and insulation rained onto Robin and me as we took a desperate dive and were caught in the edge of the fallout, driven down by our own momentum.

A second later, another crash came as the main lintels from the ceiling supporting structure came booming downward and drove what was left of the table all the way to the floor in a cloud of white chalky dust. If we'd been standing around the table two seconds longer, we'd have been killed.

Out of a wash of dusty wreckage, I pushed to my knees.

"Robin? You all right?" I pawed at the wreckage and pulled him from under a slab of ceiling board.

His face was pasty and caked with dust. "Okay . . . wow! What happened!"

Corin came crashing through the debris and lifted M'Giia out of a pile of cracked boards and support rods. "Oh, man! Are you guys all right?"

"M'Giia?" I turned to them and almost tripped. "Are you hurt?"

"No," she said with a wince as Corin set her on her feet. "No, I'm fine." Commander Chekov stumbled back toward us from the clutch of stunned cadets, all of whom now looked like ghosts of themselves, with their uniforms coated with dust. "Fine enough to explain this?"

"The Vanguard, sir," she managed. "It was the Vanguard. They decided to take action." She looked at me. "I knew that meant action against David. I'm sorry, David . . . their telepath figured out that I'd been talking to you. I guess she sensed that I was losing interest in their cause."

Chekov eyed me for a moment, then swung around to the other cadets. "All of you, clear this hall in case anything else falls. Someone contact the maintenance team and the security division. Dismissed."

He waited as they cleared the area and filed out, but he motioned for me, M'Giia, Robin and Corin to stay where we were.

When all the other cadets were gone, he turned to me.

"Well, Cadet," he said, "it looks like the next move will be yours."

"Ow . . . oh . . . mmmm . . . what a headache . . ."

I pressed my hands to my head. This might've been a whopper of a hangover, but it wasn't.

Sturek sat in a chair directly in front of me and

lowered his hands from my temples. "Fascinating," he murmured.

I moaned and rubbed my eyes. I'd heard of the Vulcan mind meld, but it was a lot weirder than anybody had ever wanted to admit. Felt like bugs crawling around the inside of my skull.

Seeming a little confused, Sturek sat back and relaxed, but he was looking at me funny.

"What's fascinating?" I asked.

"Your thoughts," he told me slowly. "Warp speed equations, dilithium ratios, navigational symbols, photon variables, women with red hair . . . and cheeseburgers."

I pushed out of my chair. "All right, just tell me if you think it worked."

He folded his arms. "There is no way to be certain until you actually infiltrate the Vanguard and their telepath scans you. The conditions will have an effect. Your level of agitation, the temperature in the room, the quality of her telepathic abilities, the depth of her training . . . all these may compromise you. How well you control your thoughts will also be a factor, as well as how long she scans you."

"But you planted a fake story?"

"I planted emotion reactions to the story you contrived. You should be able to call them up as you rethink the story. If you can do this at the right moment," he said with a warning tone, "you may deceive her."

"It's got to work, Sturek," I said. "We're both feeling the pressure of innocent lives out in space, and now I'm feeling the same thing right here at the

Academy. If M'Giia hadn't warned us, two dozen people could've been hurt or killed. Our actions have made the Vanguard up the ante. They want war with the Klingons and they'll concoct a reason on their own, if we let them."

He stood up. "Take care of yourself, David. These are dangerously obsessed people."

"I will. You keep working on the cybership. We've had more dumped in our laps than most cadets see in their first five years of active service. We have to get answers, Sturek. We've got to give Captain Kirk a reason to keep the Federation from going to war."

The Vanguard met off the campus in a former airdrome where decades ago fixed-wing buffs used to hold shows of antique aircraft. Now the place was used as a public meeting hall, and the Vanguard enjoyed particular privacy here, situated in the hills outside of the city of San Francisco. They confiscated our communications before anyone was allowed to approach the building. So I was cut off from help.

And it was weird, weird, weird to be among them. They were actually wearing robes and dark hoods. Hoods!

M'Giia came with me to the meeting, feeling the Vanguard still hoped to win her loyalty as a victim of a "Klingon" attack. They might not entirely trust her, but to have an Andorian ambassador's daughter on their side was apparently worth a risk to them. They wanted to keep working on her.

"Ow! She's giving me a headache!"

I shoved away from the Vanguard telepath as she reached out, sifting through my mind.

Frank Malan stood before M'Giia and me, armed with a phaser at his belt, and his expression said he just didn't believe that I wanted to be part of the Vanguard. I had a job on my hands.

The telepath turned to Malan. "I don't find much. I'm picking up a memory from eight years ago. His uncle, Lieutenant Allan Forester, was killed by a Klingon Bird of Prey while defending a colony. The colony was later—"

"It was handed over to the Klingons, just like Bicea," I said. "They attack and kill our people, and they get a colony for a reward. No matter what you think of me, Frank, I don't have to like what's happening any more than you do."

Malan glowered at me. "Yeah, sure! M'Giia might buy your story, Forester, but I don't. Why do you really want to join the Vanguard?"

"I wanted to join all along," I said. "I just play Starfleet's game better than you do, Frank. Captain Kirk convinced me. Once we discovered it was a new Klingon heavy cruiser behind the attacks at Bicea, he was ready to go public. But Starfleet squashed him. How can I support the Federation after that?"

"Then why did you frame Faith Gage?"

I stepped closer to him and faced him down. "That was personal and you know it. She used a member of my crew for her own purposes and she almost ruined him. She almost got Sturek killed too. What kind of a tactic is that? We can do better."

Malan's eyes narrowed with suspicion, but I could

tell he liked what he heard. Obsession was a funny thing . . . it wanted company.

Pressing another step closer, I skewered him with my most sinister glare. "The Federation wouldn't even bring up charges against the Klingons when they killed my uncle. He was just trying to defend Federation citizens, and they let him die without backup. Then they handed over the colony he'd died to defend. I'm just as sick of Federation timidity as you are. It's why I joined Starfleet in the first place—to turn back the tide before it's too late. You want to help or not?"

Other Vanguard members were gathering around us now and had heard what I said. I was careful not to look at any of them, but to glare only at Frank Malan, keeping the screws on tight and letting them know I wasn't intimidated.

Malan glared back at me, deeply suspicious but now wanting to believe. If only he didn't hate me quite as much as he hated Klingons, I'd have an edge.

He looked at the telepath, and she shook her head. "I scanned him, Frank," she said. "I think he's clear."

"I'm clear," I told them firmly. "And I can deliver something you want."

"What?" Malan challenged.

Stepping back, I now swept all the Vanguard members with a single purposeful gaze. "James T. Kirk," I told them. "He'll come if I ask him."

An excited murmur flowed across the field of hooded faces.

Something flickered in Malan's eyes—respect? I'd have settled for less.

I turned to him before it faded. "What do we do next?"

"'We' do nothing," he said, recovering some. "We'll wait until zero three hundred, one hour from now. That's when Devolution Day begins!"

A cheer rang through the hall. Now what?

"What's Devolution Day?" I asked.

"The end of the Federation as we know it."

A cold shudder rang through my chest. "How?" I croaked.

"You'll find out when it happens. The countdown's already begun. When it's over, we'll be able to place James Kirk in power as the ideal for the new society. Even if he has any lingering loyalties to the old Federation, he'll step in anyway. He's that type.'"

"Frank! Tell me what you're planning!"

Prudence should've told him to keep quiet, but Frank Malan wasn't the type to hold back. He was proud of himself as he told me, "A series of surgical assassinations at Starfleet."

My mouth dropped open. "Oh, my God . . . you're serious!"

"We're very serious. Aren't we?"

The flock of troublemakers called out in support.

"No one leaves until after the detonations!" Malan ordered. "Bar the doors! The countdown is on!"

The crowd cheered. My stomach heaved. Now what?

"You're missing an opportunity, Frank," I said, barely aware of what was going to pop out next. "You should inform Captain Kirk of your plans, so he can join in the triumph. Then he'll know there's no turning back, and he'll accept your loyalty."

Several of the other Vanguard members crowded closer, fascinated by the prospect of getting James Kirk on their side. They saw me as the link.

Malan contemplated what I'd said, but the doubt lingered behind his gaze.

"Good idea." He handed me a standard issue Starfleet hand communicator. "You get Kirk over here. Right now, before the fireworks start. Then, I'll believe whatever you say."

M'Giia watched me, wide-eyed. As I opened the communicator's grid, Malan drew his phaser and put it to M'Giia's head.

Simple enough. Message received.

Knotted up like a braid, I raised the communicator to my lips.

"Captain Kirk . . . this is Cadet Forester. I have special information. Come in, please . . ."

Chapter 18

"I just can't bring myself to trust you, Forester. Where is he?"

"He said he'd come, Malan."

"So what takes so long!"

Frank Malan looked at his telepath, but she continued to shake her head and shrug.

Malan had said there was an hour before "Devolution Day," whatever they meant by that. Reactionaries—everything had to have a name. Bet they were proud of themselves for calling their petty destruction something other than petty destruction.

Now forty-two minutes had passed. Forty-three. Only seventeen minutes before bombs started going off in key quarters around Starfleet and key people started dying.

It was inconceivable! I was starting to notice how sheltered I'd been in my life. I'd never been around people who wanted to kill anyone else before. A full forty minutes had gone by before I really believed them.

But their nervous excitement was telling, and M'Giia's silent eyes betrayed the fact that she believed every word. She had known enough misery and loss in her life that she knew the real thing when it came near her. They meant to kill.

Their countdown was being ticked off on a portable computer unit that looked as if it had been hijacked from the Academy—probably Frank Malan's personal contribution—settled in the center of the room, surrounded by nervous Vanguarders.

I was entertaining thoughts of rushing Malan and that phaser he held on M'Giia, when a clack came at the wide barn doors of the airdrome and the telepath rushed to open the door.

Holding my breath, I hoped—yes! Captain Kirk strode in, all alone.

The whole room fell to silence. Kirk stood at the door, unimpressed by the throng of reactionaries.

He started toward us. The only sound was the click of his boots on the hard concrete floor.

Just when he would've come nearly to my side, he veered away and faced the whole roomful of Vanguarders.

"I hear there's a group here ready to take on the Klingons!"

He sounded rousing, angry, and the crowd reacted with a roar of applause and cheers. They'd suddenly gone from a splinter group to a powerful body with credibility.

"Sir!" Malan addressed him, pushing M'Giia away. "Your presence means victory to us!"

Kirk turned to him in his famous no-nonsense way and said, "Get to the point. What's your plan?"

"Sir, we've set up explosives in the offices of key Starfleet officials. Once those reluctant to act against the Klingons and Romulans are gone, we're ready to step in and restore order immediately! You'll be presiding over a new Federation!"

"You better have placed your bombs well," Kirk said blandly. "Federation security is no joke. Let's see your layout."

Malan rushed to the computer table and scooped up a padd and handed it to Kirk. Kirk surveyed the information. He still hadn't looked at me or even acknowledged that I was here.

"Let's see . . . looks good . . . oh, yes, I've wanted to get rid of that guy for a while now . . . incendiaries planted in Starfleet Security, Planetary Defense, and the Federation Council—very thorough. And H-hour is fifteen minutes from now. You people have guts, Malan. I underestimated you."

"Thank you, Captain! We're honored, sir!"

"Good for you."

Kirk glanced around, then tossed the padd to me. "Take a look, Forester. You might learn something."

The padd landed in my hands, and Kirk instantly swung away from me and started strolling toward the other side of the room, drawing with him the eyes of every Vanguard idiot in the place.

"You know what we're fighting for?" he began, with

fire in his delivery. "You know what the stakes are in a galaxy filled with murderers?"

I clutched the padd and sidled toward the computer set-up.

"Ever since the Organian Peace Treaty," Kirk went on, loudly and forcefully, "the Federation has been a wolf with no fangs. Hostile aliens nip at our heels and we cower back. Every day of peace brings us closer to the end of the Federation as we know it. And what do we do about it?"

Keeping my eyes on the padd, I edged up to the computer and tapped the remote access key, which connected the countdown sequence into the padd.

Just a few seconds . . . the timer sequences began scrolling on the padd's screen.

Kirk's voice continued ringing through the hall. He kept moving, never letting anyone settle their attention, creating a moving attraction for those who were infatuated by his presence.

"More shore leave for our enemies on Starfleet bases! More unaligned worlds brutalized by foreign landing parties! I say enough! You are the new blood that will stand up to interstellar assassins!"

The Vanguard cheered wildly, intoxicated by the smell of power and a bloodlust I just couldn't understand.

"Traitor!"

A vicious scream pierced my ears from very close. The telepath was pointing at me, and the attention of the hall shifted from Kirk to me.

"He's trying to stop the countdown!"

She plunged forward and snatched the padd out of my hands.

"He blew out the timers! We're ruined!"

Malan bellowed, "I knew he was lying!" He speared his telepath with a glare. "How'd he fool your probes?"

"I don't know! He can't—" Then her face changed and she wailed, "His science officer is a Vulcan! They must've set up a temporary shield!"

Well, the cover was blown. I swung around. "Go, M'Giia!"

I shoved M'Giia out of the center of the crowd toward a wall, though there was no place to go from there. At least we wouldn't be surrounded.

The telepath threw down the padd and drew her phaser, but M'Giia kicked wildly and knocked the telepath's arm out of aim just as the phaser went off. The bolt seared the wall, and the phaser tumbled from the telepath's hand.

I lashed out and knocked down the nearest Vanguarder, but two more rushed in to replace him and they were rushing us.

"Any ideas?" M'Giia gasped.

"You take the first dozen, I'll take the second—"

My miserable attempt at defiance was met by a boot in the chest. I hit the wall and came back slugging. Malan appeared out of the crowd, his face a quilt of anger, and he drove his knee upward into my midsection. I was thrown hard, my lungs were heaving. Doubled and completely winded, I staggered against the wall and tried to fend off the Vanguard, but there were nearly fifty of them in here and only the two of us. In seconds, M'Giia and I were tackled.

"The bombs!" The telepath choked out her fury. "What happened to the bombs!"

Frank Malan was crouched in front of the computer remote, his face twisting in rage. "They're shut down! He blew the timers!"

Storming toward me, he let fly a backhanded slap that set my head ringing.

"Tell me how to fix them, you traitorous bastard!"

Dazed, I glared at him and actually smiled past a bruised lip. "Fix them yourself, you self-righteous maniac."

His teeth ground together and he boiled with anger. I figured I was dead, but Malan didn't hit me again. Instead he drew his phaser and spun it to M'Giia's head. "The alien invader dies first! How do you like this, Forester!"

"Hold it!" The sharp voice of James Kirk cut through the hall.

The captain came slowly through the surprised Vanguard.

Disillusioned, Malan turned and pointed his phaser at Kirk. "Please . . . don't tell me you're a traitor too."

"Not likely," Kirk said. "Forester lied to you, but he betrayed me first. If you want me to be your leader, his punishment is my call, not yours."

Malan held the phaser up, but his jaw worked with unsureness. His arms quivered and his legs shifted back and forth as he tried to decide what do to, who to trust, but for one who was so bad at trusting, such decisions came hard. He didn't know what to do.

The fiery eyes of James Kirk never left Malan's. The steady gaze was disarming for the idealistic, if misled, young cadet.

I knew the feeling—I'd have followed James Kirk off a cliff in those few moments if he'd asked me. He was like a magician rising from smoke and hypnotizing us, and Frank suddenly looked very, very young.

"Yes . . ." Malan's voice was barely a scratch. "Yes, Captain!"

Kirk held out his hand. At first Malan didn't seem to understand, but then realized that Kirk was asking for the phaser.

Overwhelmed, he handed the phaser to Kirk, and the captain turned the weapon on me.

With the rest of the Vanguard standing behind him, James Kirk aimed the weapon squarely at my chest.

He extended the weapon as if he were about to shoot, then paused.

"This isn't set to kill," he said.

Malan blinked. "It's not?"

Kirk slowly pivoted away, fiddling with the phaser. "Why kill when I can . . . wide angle stun?"

He raised the weapon and fired, this time facing the entire squadron of Vanguarders. The whole roomful of robed nuts collapsed in a single purple heap!

Malan had been standing near me, out of the line of fire, and now made a crazy dive for the telepath's phaser and scooped the weapon from her unconscious body. He fumbled briefly, then stood up in the midst of his collapsed fellows, and raised his weapon.

He looked up in time to see James Kirk's phaser aimed squarely at his head.

"Put the phaser down, Mr. Malan."

It was a standoff.

Malan was ringing wet with sweat now, his plans destroyed, his hero betraying him, and his career in shreds.

"Put it down, Frank," I said. "The Vanguard's finished."

Kirk moved slowly toward him, phaser aim never wavering. "I could stun you," he said, "but I'd rather you make a decision."

I wanted to believe, and any good cadet would, that this was just the power of James Kirk's mighty legend at work, but oddly I saw something completely different in Kirk's own eyes. He knew there was more going on, perhaps that Frank Malan was an idealist and an enraptured young man whose beliefs had gotten the better of him, but that when it came down to actually pulling a phaser trigger, actually doing the killing himself with his own hands, the power necessary from the human soul was something Frank just didn't possess.

I learned a lot in those few seconds, about Frank, about myself, about conviction, and about James Kirk. He was even smarter than his legend.

Then again, the legend was in our minds. Captain Kirk was really here.

Malan was both confused and overpowered by the intensity of Kirk's conviction. Up against that, Malan's petty ambitions didn't have a chance.

Destruction of the soul, however, could be too much to bear.

Malan cracked, yes, but not the way I expected. He turned his phaser away from James Kirk, and put it to his own head.

Kirk paused an instant, then walked toward Malan, and he lowered his own phaser. What an incredible move . . . he might as well have dropped his own weapon!

He reached out to Frank like a stern parent. He said absolutely nothing. The only voice in the wide room was that of Kirk's strength of will.

Broken and humiliated, Malan sank to one knee. His phaser fell away from his own skull. As James Kirk approached him, Frank Malan was a destroyed young man.

And sad it was to see.

Sad for me, to watch a fellow cadet go down under the weight of his own misconceptions, so far removed from everything Starfleet stood for. Maybe in some ways Frank was right, maybe we should be stronger, but his methods were all wrong. We couldn't go jumping to violent solutions at warp speed. How could anyone ever trust us if we did?

How could we trust each other?

As Malan wept at his feet, James Kirk turned to me. "Hurt?"

I sucked a hard breath into my tortured middle and managed to say, "Yah . . . it hurts."

But I smiled around it.

Kirk scanned the scene, satisfied. Then he opened his communicator. "Kirk to Starfleet Security. Transport two teams to these coordinates. We have . . . looks like about fifty conspirators to take into custody."

"Starfleet Security, acknowledged, Captain. We'll be right there."

M'Giia came to stand beside me, and she looked more satisfied and fulfilled than I'd ever seen her, as if she'd somehow avenged her lost family by saving the lives of others. That was a nice feeling, for both of us.

"Nice work disarming the bombs, Mr. Forester," Kirk said as he took charge of Frank's phaser. "So much for another no-win scenario. Now you see why I don't believe in them."

"Sir," I rasped, "I'm beginning not to believe in them either!"

"Good job. Don't be too satisfied, though."

"Sir?"

"You're not done. You and Mr. Sturek are going to throw your analysis into high warp. We've cut out the core of the Vanguard, but the Klingons are still angry about these activities and someone is still attacking outposts. People are still dying, Forester. It's up to us to find out who, and stop them."

Chapter 19

"I don't understand. We've got several different fragments, but they all contain the same set of etched structures."

"Apparently there are old pathways and new pathways in the metal, with some that have been overwritten or blocked off."

"If I were a scientist, like you, that might not tell me anything. But I'm a pilot, and it tells me a lot. It suggests that something actually goes down those paths."

"David, they are simply too small. Only basic subatomic particles would be able to travel down these. There would be problems controlling the matrix."

"Let's find out anyway."

That was what fatigue would get you—crazy guesses. Nothing could go down the things, so Sturek and I were looking anyway. The etchings on the bits of junk from the new attack ship were meticulously engineered on the molecular level. It wasn't just random crystallization. That meant intelligence, not just a random attack by a big dumb being that looked like a ship. We weren't dealing with a galactic grizzly bear here.

Sturek was exhausted, even though he wasn't admitting it. His voice was thready, his movements sluggish, but he was driven to find the key to the cybership. I knew he felt responsible for the loss of the first set of data, despite the fact that "logically" he had nothing to do with that.

"No measurable change," he said dully after our—how many experiments was this?

No, I didn't want to count anymore.

"The results for protons and neutrons are the same. The simulation has failed."

Poor Sturek. I was letting him down. I wasn't being original enough or crazy enough or something—I had to be more creative. That wasn't in his bag of tricks, so it had to be in mine.

"I'm not willing to accept that. This thing is intelligent and that means communication. We've got to find a way to talk to it. What if we try antielectrons?"

He shook his head wearily. "The matrix would explode. Matter can't exist with antimatter."

"So it explodes. What've we got to lose?"

He dragged his hands back to the console and arranged another piece of the fragment into the analyzer. "First, antiprotons."

The analyzer hummed, and then the plate exploded, blowing shredded pea-sized bits all over Sturek.

"Sorry . . . you okay?" I asked.

He brushed the splintered junk off his cheek. "Yes. As expected."

"Try the antielectrons. But look—try it this way. Set it up to mimic the cybernetic patterns. Let's see what it does with something it recognizes."

Sturek blinked up at me. "What is the logic for that?"

"Well, if I want to speak to something, I speak in something it already knows, don't I? Let's see if it responds."

"David, any sentience may be an illusion. They could be cosmic parrots."

"Parrots don't build starships. And they don't attack colonies. This thing has a brain and I'm going to find it."

Maybe he was tired, maybe he just didn't understand my stab in the dark, but he shrugged and tapped the computer console, feeding in my wild attempt to talk to the cybership's bits. This was like having one brain cell from a human being and trying to see if it spoke English. All we had to do was get a positive response, and Captain Kirk would be justified in demanding that Starfleet's supergeniuses take it from there and find a way to communicate.

Who the hell are you and why are you attacking outposts?

"David . . . David!"

Vulcan reserve hit the floor. Sturek jolted back and stared at the readout screen.

Lights and neural responses scrolled wildly.

"It recognized the pattern!" I cried. "It's answering! Sturek, we did it! It's not a spoken language, but there is a sentient pattern! That's the trick—we can't make it follow corporeal thinking, so we have to imitate its thought process! By mimicking a cybership's every move, a Federation ship can develop a rapport! Come on! We've got to get this to Captain Kirk!"

"It is my honor and privilege to award Cadet David Ross Forester with the Commandant's Medal of Meritorious Service and the Starfleet Call of Duty Award. I now confer upon you the rank of second lieutenant. Congratulations, Mr. Forester."

Cheers rose to the prisms of the ceremonial hall at Starfleet Academy, but I heard only the first surge of noise before my brain went a little numb.

The field of cadets applauding me were in full dress for graduation. In the front row, in positions of honor, sitting with Captain Kirk, Captain Sulu, and Commander Chekov, were my crew—Corin, M'Giia, Jana, Robin, and Sturek. We were officers now.

I looked at my crew and nodded. I was especially proud to see Sturek wearing his Commandant's Medal of Achievement. He deserved it.

In spite of our success, I keenly felt the stinging absence of Frank Malan and Faith Gage, much more than I'd expected to. Their dismissal had busted the chances of a ten-year no-expulsion record for Starfleet Academy, and I knew I'd had a hand in that. Oh, sure, they'd probably have caused a lot more trouble if I hadn't gummed up their works, but still I felt saddened that the whole episode had to happen and regretful that I had to be part of it.

The two-story windows crackled with sunlight off San Francisco Bay as Commandant Rotherot clipped the medals to my uniform and shook my hand.

"Lieutenant," he said, "report to docking bay twelve at eight hundred hours. Your entire crew will be there waiting for you."

"My crew, sir?"

"Yes. It doesn't happen very often, but your entire command team has turned down their postings to continue serving with their training captain. Congratulations, David."

Astonished, I looked down at Corin, Robin, Jana, M'Giia and Sturek. They seemed to know he'd just told me that.

And all the feelings of regret fell away.

"Docking bay twelve, eight hundred hours. I'll be there, sir. We'll all be there!"

"This way, Mr. Forester. You'd better learn the route."

My legs were scarcely more than twists of thread as James Kirk led me into the one place in the universe I'd never expected to be standing—the bridge of the *Starship Enterprise*.

This was the real starship, right here, hovering in her box dock, which glittered outside the main screen like a Christmas decoration. Hovering here in elegant repose as we'd all come in on the docking shuttle, the starship glowed under the work lights like a swan in starshine.

And the first thing I noticed as we walked onto the bridge was the scent of the place—not like the simulator at all. The simulator smelled musty and sooty because of the frequent blasting that went on inside it. This place had a light aroma of tidiness, of freshly polished bulkheads and vacuumed carpet. That's what happened to the starship every time she made port. Her crew—not maintenance from the starbase, but her own crew—cleaned her up and made her shipshape before embarking for shore leave.

Suddenly I wanted to buff something.

"She's been in spacedock for six weeks now, and she's ready for a shakedown," Captain Kirk said casually, speaking about the great ship as if she were his favorite riding horse.

"Mr. Sturek, right over there. Ensigns Corin and Akton, the helm . . . Ensign M'Giia, communications . . . Mr. Brady, main engineering is right over there."

I was shaken from my amazement by the sight in my periphery of Robin coming past me and running his fingers along the engineering console of the big ship. On my right, Sturek stood at the science station, not touching it at all. It was as if he stood in a museum, appreciating the work of a great master.

I smiled. I knew what he was feeling.

Then it hit me again—this wasn't the simulator!

Chekov and Sulu came in after my crew, fondly touching the equipment, right at home here. My crew, though, wasn't sure at all what to do. They responded politely when spoken to, but we all were a little drugged.

"Once around the solar system, Mr. Forester," Captain Kirk said then, dropping to my side next to the command chair.

Stunned, I turned to look at him. "Sir?"

He waved his hand toward space on the main screen. "Take her out, shake her down, and then come back and pick me up in the morning. But be aware, if you bring her back with so much as a scratch, I'll file your ears to points."

Was he talking about . . .

He took my elbow then and almost scared me out of my skin.

"Right there, Mr. Forester. The command chair."

He gestured to the all-important place as I stared in bald shock. Take the command chair?

Behind him, Sulu and Chekov were grinning.

"Thanks to you," Kirk said, "we know how to communicate with the cybership. Your work with Mr. Sturek is paying off. Tomorrow we're going out to deal with the crisis. You started this mission, and it's up to you to finish it."

Overwhelmed, drawing strength from the supportive gazes of my own crew, I stepped up onto the command platform and lowered into the command chair as if it were hot and sizzling.

"This is an honor, sir," I struggled.

Kirk didn't smile, exactly, but he held out his hand to me and clasped mine with unexpected warmth. Around us, the beautiful bridge shone, and its crews, past and future, beamed with pride as the torch was passed.

On the bridge of the *U.S.S. Enterprise,* flagship of

the United Federation of Planets, of which I was now a representative, Captain James T. Kirk clasped my hand a second longer than was necessary. He spoke to me with a resonance that would carry through my life in Starfleet, as ever long that would someday be . . .

"Wherever you go," he said, "go boldly."

COMING IN JULY!

STAR TREK®

VULCAN'S FORGE

by
Josepha Sherman and Susan Shwartz

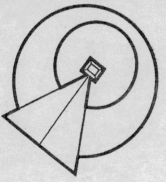

Please turn the page for an excerpt from

Vulcan's Forge . . .

Intrepid II and Obsidian,
Day 4, Fifth Week, Month of the Raging *Durak*,
Year 2296

Lieutenant Duchamps, staring at the sight of Obsidian growing ever larger in the viewscreen, pursed his lips in a silent whistle. "Would you look at that. . . ."

Captain Spock, who had been studying the viewscreen as well, glanced quickly at the helmsman. "Lieutenant?"

Duchamps, predictably, went back into too-formal mode at this sudden attention. "The surface of Obsidian, sir. I was thinking how well-named it is, sir. All those sheets of that black volcanic glass glittering in the sun. Sir."

"That black volcanic glass is, indeed, what constitutes the substance known as obsidian," Spock observed, though only someone extremely familiar with Vulcans—James Kirk, for instance—could have read any dry humor into his matter-of-fact voice. Getting to his feet, Spock added to Uhura, "I am leaving for the transporter room, Commander. You have the conn."

"Yes, sir."

He waited to see her seated in the command chair, knowing how important this new role was to her, then acknowledged Uhura's right to be there with the smallest of nods. She solemnly nodded back, aware that he had just offered her silent congratulations. But Uhura being Uhura, she added in quick mischief, "Now, don't forget to write!"

After so many years among humans, Spock knew perfectly well that this was meant as a good-natured, tongue-in-cheek farewell, but he obligingly retorted, "I see no reason why I should utilize so inappropriate a means of communication," and was secretly gratified to see Uhura's grin.

He was less gratified at the gasps of shock from the rest of the bridge crew. Did they not see the witticism as such? Or were they shocked that Uhura could dare be so familiar? Spock firmly blocked a twinge of very illogical nostalgia; illogical, he told himself, because the past was exactly that.

McCoy was waiting for him, for once silent on the subject of "having my molecules scattered all over Creation." With the doctor were several members of Security and a few specialists, such as the friendly, sensible Lieutenant Clayton, an agronomist, and the efficient young Lieutenant Diver, a geologist so new to Starfleet that her insignia still looked like they'd just come out of the box. Various other engineering and medical personnel would be following later. The heaviest of the doctor's supplies had already been beamed down with other equipment, but he stubbornly clung to the medical satchel—his "little black bag," as McCoy so anachronistically called it—slung over his shoulder.

"I decided to go," he told Spock unnecessarily. "That outrageously high rate of skin cancer and lethal mutations makes it a fascinating place."

That seemingly pure-science air, Spock mused, fooled no one. No doctor worthy of the title could turn away from so many hurting people.

"Besides," McCoy added acerbically, "someone's got to make sure you all wear your sunhats."

"Indeed. Energize," Spock commanded, and . . .

. . . was elsewhere, from the unpleasantly cool, relatively dim ship—cool and dim to Vulcan senses, at any rate—to the dazzlingly bright light and welcoming heat of Obsidian. The veils instantly slid down over Spock's eyes, then up again as his desert-born vision adapted, while the humans hastily adjusted their sun visors. He glanced about at this new world, seeing a flat, gravelly surface, tan-brown-gray stretching to the horizon of jagged, clearly volcanic peaks. A hot wind teased grit and sand into miniature spirals, and the sun glinted off shards of the black volcanic glass that had given this world its Federation name.

"Picturesque," someone commented wryly, but Spock ignored that. Humans, he knew, used sarcasm to cover uneasiness. Or perhaps it was discomfort; perhaps they felt the higher level of ionization in the air as he did, prickling at their skin.

No matter. One accepted what could not be changed. They had, at David Rabin's request, beamed down to these coordinates a distance away from the city: "The locals are uneasy enough as it is without a sudden 'invasion' in their midst."

Logical. And there was the Federation detail he had been told to expect, at its head a sturdy, familiar figure: David Rabin. He stepped forward, clad in a standard Federation hot-weather outfit save for his decidedly non-standard-issue headgear of some loose, flowing material caught by a circle of corded rope. Sensible, Spock thought, to adapt what was clearly an effective local solution to the problem of sunstroke.

"Rabin of Arabia," McCoy muttered, but Spock let that pass. Captain Rabin, grinning widely, was offering him the split-fingered Vulcan Greeting of the Raised Hand and saying, "Live long and prosper."

There could be no response but one. Spock returned the salutation and replied simply, "Shalom."

This time McCoy had nothing to say.

It was only a short drive to the outpost. "Solar-powered vehicles, of course," Rabin noted. "No shortage of solar power on this world! The locals don't really mind our getting around like this as long as we don't bring any vehicles into Kalara or frighten the *chuchaki*—those cameloid critters over there."

Spock forbore to criticize the taxonomy.

Kalara, he mused, looked very much the standard desert city to be found on many low-tech, and some high-tech, worlds. Mud brick really was the most practical organic building material, and thick walls and high windows provided quite efficient passive air cooling. Kalara was, of course, an oasis town; he didn't need to see the oasis to extrapolate that conclusion. No desert city came into being without a steady, reliable source of water and, therefore, a steady, reliable source of food. Spock noted the tips of some feathery green branches peeking over the high walls and nodded. Good planning for both economic and safety reasons to have some of that reliable water source be within the walls. Add to that the vast underground network of irrigation canals and wells, and these people were clearly doing a clever job of exploiting their meager resources.

Or would be, were it not for that treacherous sun.

And, judging from what Rabin had already warned, for that all too common problem in times of crisis: fanaticism.

It is illogical, he thought, for any one person or persons to claim to know a One True Path to enlightenment. And I must, he added honestly, include my own distant ancestors in that thought.

And, he reluctantly added, some Vulcans not so far removed in time.

"What's *that?*" McCoy exclaimed suddenly. "Hebrew graffiti?"

"Deuteronomy," Rabin replied succinctly, adding, "We're home, everybody."

They left the vehicles and entered the Federation outpost, and in the process made a jarring jump from timelessness to gleaming modernity. Spock paused only an instant at the shock of what to him was a wall of unwelcome coolness; around him, the humans were all breathing sighs of relief. McCoy put down his shoulder pack with a grunt. "Hot as Vulcan out there."

"Just about," Rabin agreed cheerfully, pulling off his native headgear. "And if you think this is bad, wait till Obsidian's summer. This sun, good old unstable Loki, will kill you quite efficiently.

"Please, everyone, relax for a bit. Drink something even if you don't feel thirsty. It's ridiculously easy to dehydrate here, especially when none of you are desert acclimated. Or rather," he added before Spock could comment, "when even the desert-born among you haven't been *in* any deserts for a while. While you're resting, I'll fill you in on what's been happening here."

Quickly and efficiently, Rabin set out the various problems—the failed hydroponics program, the beetles, the mysterious fires and spoiled supply dumps. When he was finished, Spock noted, "One, two or even three incidents might be considered no more than unpleasant coincidence. But taken as a whole, this series of incidents can logically only add up to deliberate sabotage."

"Which is what I was thinking," Rabin agreed. "'One's accident, two's coincidence, three's enemy action,' or however the quote goes. The trouble is: Who *is* the enemy? Or rather, which one?"

Spock raised an eyebrow ever so slightly. "These are, if the records are indeed correct, a desert people with a relatively low level of technology."

"They are that. And before you ask, no, there's absolutely no trace of Romulan or any other off-world involvement."

"Then we need ask: Who of this world would have sufficient organization and initiative to work such an elaborate scheme of destruction?"

The human sighed. "Who, indeed? We've got a good many local dissidents; we both know how many nonconformists a desert can breed. But none of the local brand of agitators could ever band together long enough to mount a definite threat. They hate each other as much or maybe even more than they hate us."

"And in the desert?"

"Ah, Spock, old buddy, just how much manpower do you think I have? Much as I'd love to up and search all that vastness—"

"It would mean leaving the outpost unguarded. I understand."

"Besides," Rabin added thoughtfully, "I can't believe that any of the desert people, even the 'wild nomads,' as the folks in Kalara call the deep-desert tribes, would do anything to destroy precious resources, even those from off-world. They might destroy *us,* but not food or water."

"Logic," Spock retorted, "requires that someone is working this harm. Whether you find the subject pleasant or not, *someone* is 'poisoning the wells.'"

"Excuse me, sir," Lieutenant Clayton said, "but wouldn't it be relatively simple for the *Intrepid* to do a scan of the entire planet?"

"It could—"

"But that," Rabin cut in, "wouldn't work. The trouble is those 'wild nomads' are a pain in the . . . well, they're a nuisance to find by scanning because they tend to hide out against solar flares. And where they hide is in hollows shielded by rock that's difficult or downright impossible for scanners to penetrate. We have no idea how many nomads are out there, nor do the city folk. Oh, and if that wasn't enough," he added wryly, "the high level of ionization in the atmosphere, thank you very much Loki, provides a high amount of static to signal."

Spock moved to the banks of equipment set up to measure ionization, quickly scanning the data. "The levels do fluctuate within the percentages of possibility. A successful scan is unlikely but not improbable during the lower ranges of the scale. We will attempt one. I have a science officer who will regard this as a personal challenge." As do I, he added silently. A Vulcan could, after all, assemble the data far more swiftly than a human who— No. McCoy had quite wisely warned him against "micromanaging." He was not what he had been, Spock reminded himself severely. And only an emotional being longed for what had been and was no more.

Look for STAR TREK Fiction from Pocket Books

Star Trek®: The Original Series

Star Trek: The Next Generation®

Encounter at Farpoint • David Gerrold
Unification • Jeri Taylor
Relics • Michael Jan Friedman
Descent • Diane Carey
All Good Things • Michael Jan Friedman
Star Trek: Klingon • Dean W. Smith & Kristine K. Rusch
Star Trek VII: Generations • J. M. Dillard
Metamorphosis • Jean Lorrah
Vendetta • Peter David
Reunion • Michael Jan Friedman
Imzadi • Peter David
The Devil's Heart • Carmen Carter
Dark Mirror • Diane Duane
Q-Squared • Peter David
Crossover • Michael Jan Friedman
Kahless • Michael Jan Friedman
Star Trek: First Contact • J. M. Dillard

Star Trek: Deep Space Nine®

Star Trek®: Voyager™

**It is the Day of Reckoning
It is the Day of Judgment
It is . . .**

STAR TREK

THE DAY OF HONOR

**A Four-Part Klingon Saga
That Spans the Generations**

**Coming Summer '97
from Pocket Books**

STAR TREK
THE DAY OF HONOR

A Four-Part Klingon Saga

Coming Summer '97
from Pocket Books

Following the overwhelmingly popular **STAR TREK: INVASION!** series (over 1,000,000 copies in print), next spring Pocket Books will present **STAR TREK: THE DAY OF HONOR,** a four-part series centered around the most important Klingon holiday.

To a true Klingon warrior, no occasion is more sacred than **The Day of Honor,** the day when he must reflect on his own honor and that of his enemies. But honor always exacts its price.

The story begins in *Star Trek: The Next Generation:* **ANCIENT BLOOD** by Diane Carey (creator of **STAR TREK: INVASION!**), continues in *Star Trek: Deep Space Nine:* **ARMAGEDDON SKY** by L. A. Graf and *Star Trek: Voyager:* **HER KLINGON SOUL** by Michael Jan Friedman, and concludes in *Star Trek: The Original Series:* **TREATY'S LAW** by Dean Wesley Smith and Kristine Kathryn Rusch, which tells the story of the founding of The Day of Honor.

STAR TREK
THE DAY OF HONOR

THE DAY OF HONOR

Book One of Four

ANCIENT BLOOD
by
Diane Carey

Worf finds his honor tested when he goes undercover to infiltrate a planetary criminal network. How can he root out the corruption on New Delphi without resorting to deceit and treachery himself? Worf's dilemma is shared by his son, Alexander, who is searching for the true meaning of honor in the human side of his heritage. Along with his son, Worf must confront deadly danger that threatens far more than just his life.

STAR TREK
THE DAY OF HONOR

ON SALE IN MID-AUGUST

STAR TREK
DEEP SPACE NINE®
THE DAY OF HONOR

Book Two of Four

ARMAGEDDON SKY

by

L. A. Graf

A hunded years ago he was Commander Kor of the Klingon Empire, and one of the founders of The Day of Honor. Now, having thrown away the Sword of Kahless, he is nothing but a harmless old man—or is he? While Dax and Bashir fight to save a colony of Klingons banished to Cardassian territory for their loyalty to Worf's family, Worf and Kor must face the hard choices that their honor has led them into.

STAR TREK
THE DAY OF HONOR

ON SALE IN MID-SEPTEMBER

THE DAY OF HONOR

Book Three of Four

HER KLINGON SOUL

by

Michael Jan Friedman

Even light-years from the Klingon Empire, The Day of Honor is known. And sometimes honor is found in the most unlikely places.

Lieutenant B'Elanna Torres has never cared for The Day of Honor. The holiday is an unwelcome reminder of the Klingon heritage she has tried to repress. But when Torres and Ensign Harry Kim are captured by alien slavers and forced to mine deadly radioactive ore, B'Elanna will need all her strength and cunning to survive—and her honor as well.

STAR TREK
THE DAY OF HONOR

ON SALE IN MID-SEPTEMBER

THE DAY OF HONOR

Book Four of Four

TREATY'S LAW
by
**Dean Wesley Smith and
Kristine Kathryn Rusch**

By the time of *Star Trek: The Next Generation,* The Day of Honor is celebrated throughout the Klingon Empire. But every tradition has its starting place.

Signi Beta is an M-Class planet ideal for farming. The terms of the Organian peace treaty have given the planet to the Klingon Empire. Captain Kirk is not happy to lose this world to Commander Kor, his frequent enemy. But when a mysterious fleet attacks both the Klingons and the *Enterprise,* Kirk and Kor must rely on each other's honor—or neither of them will live through the day.